Maine Men Book Five

Shaun's
SALVATION

K.C. WELLS

Shaun's Salvation
Copyright © 2021 by K.C. Wells
Cover Art by Meredith Russell
Edited by Sue Laybourn

Warning
This book contains material that is intended for a mature, adult audience. It contains graphic language, explicit sexual content, and adult situations.

<u>Maine Men</u>
Levi, Noah, Aaron, Ben, Dylan, Finn, Seb, and Shaun.
Eight friends who met in high school in Wells, Maine.
Different backgrounds, different paths, but one thing remains solid, even eight years after they graduated – their friendship. Holidays, weddings, funerals, birthdays, parties – any chance they get to meet up, they take it. It's an opportunity to share what's going on in their lives, especially their love lives.

Back in high school, they knew four of them were gay or bi, so maybe it was more than coincidence that they gravitated to one another. Along the way, there were revelations and realizations, some more of a surprise than others. And what none of the others knew was that Levi was in love with one of them…

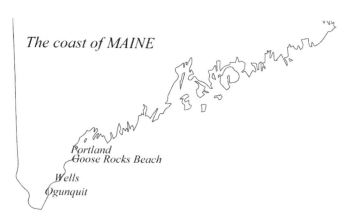

The coast of MAINE

Portland
Goose Rocks Beach
Wells
Ogunquit

Prologue

From Dylan's Dilemma

Dylan studied him. "You were very quiet tonight." It didn't take a genius to work out why.

Shaun focused on his bottle. "Yeah. Things... things aren't good right now. Christ, I was so torn about this weekend. I haven't been away from Dad since Grammy's birthday party in June, and you have *no* idea how much I needed this. But at the same time..." He swallowed. "Not that he'll realize I've been gone."

"Is it that bad?" Dylan knew very little about dementia.

"I think he's reached stage six. I wasn't sure how long it would be before we got there, but it kinda came at us like a Mack truck."

"What's stage six?"

Shaun sighed. "You don't want to hear about this."

"Maybe not, but it seems to me that you *need* to talk about it. And I talked *your* ear off enough times when we were seniors, so I think I can be here for you now." Shaun and the others had been Dylan's lifeline, his refuge from the passive-aggressive prison he'd lived in.

Not that I knew back then what passive-aggressive even meant. Realization had come later.

Shaun took a long drink of water before speaking. "I know more about dementia than I ever wanted to. There are seven stages, and six of them all have the words *cognitive decline* in their title. The thing is, there's no rhyme or reason as to how fast a person moves between stages. So many factors have to be taken into account." Another drink. "He'd been at stage five for a long time. That was when he needed help dressing and bathing. That was also when I employed the first in-home nurse."

"Didn't you tell us about his new in-home nurse? It's a guy, right?"

Shaun nodded. "Nathan. He's great. I couldn't cope without him."

"So what's different about stage six?"

Shaun's face tightened. "Then, he was getting more and more confused or forgetful. But now…Dad's not sleeping well. He gets into these… loops of obsessive behavior, like when he wants to tell me about something that happened forty years ago when he was a teenager, but he tells the same story over and over." He swallowed. "He has these bursts of paranoia, and he won't listen when I tell him everything's fine. It feels like he's always worrying about something. And…" There was pain in Shaun's eyes, and Dylan ached to see it. "Last week, he… he looked right at me and said 'Who are you?'" He lowered his gaze. "This is what they call Severe Cognitive Decline, and suddenly we're only one step away from Very Severe. And when *that* happens…"

Dylan couldn't speak. There was nothing he could say to ease Shaun's suffering, and he didn't want to offer trite words. His face tingled. *I'm sitting here, worrying if I'm missing out on stuff, and meanwhile, Shaun is going through hell.* It put Dylan's feelings into sharp relief.

"How about we try to get some sleep?" he

suggested. "Because you *know* Aaron will be up with the birds, making breakfast and demanding we all get out of bed. And then it'll be no time at all before Seb is grilling up a storm for lunch."

Shaun's sad smile made his stomach clench. "I wasn't sure about staying for lunch, to be honest. We'll see. But you're right. We should try to get a few hours' sleep."

Dylan picked up his phone and followed him out of the kitchen, both of them creeping into the living room. He climbed beneath the sheets, and Shaun got in on the other side. On impulse, Dylan reached across and found Shaun's arm. He squeezed it. "I know there's nothing I can say that will make your situation any better," he whispered, "but... if you ever need me—whether it's just a chat on the phone, or even a hotel room for the night when you need a break—I'm here for you. Okay?"

Shaun's hand covered his. "Thanks, man. I really do appreciate it."

Dylan lay on his back, listening to the change in Shaun's breathing as he finally fell asleep. *Poor guy.* Shaun had a hard row to hoe: once his dad had started along this path, they'd all known it was going to be a downward slope, one that would lead to an unhappy ending. And all they could do was be there for him.

Chapter One

October 31

Shaun Clark watched his dad from the living room archway. Dad was in his recliner, the one he called all-singin'-n-dancin' because of its many functions. He was staring at the TV, but Shaun doubted he was paying attention to the movie.

Where does he go to, in those moments when it's obvious his mind is somewhere else?

Then Dad turned his head and stared at Shaun, his brow furrowed. "Tell your mom to make me some French toast, would ya?"

Shaun swallowed. There was little use telling him Mom had passed away nine years ago. "Sure, Dad." He went into the kitchen. Nathan was due any minute, but Shaun had time to make French toast. He broke an egg into a shallow dish, then added vanilla and cinnamon. He was pouring the milk in when Nathan arrived at the back door. "Hey," Shaun greeted him as he came into the warm kitchen. "Just making Dad some French toast. Want some?"

Nathan smiled. "You don't have to do that." He removed his coat and hung it by the door.

Shaun gestured to the carton of eggs and the slices of bread. "There's plenty."

"I won't say no then." Nathan glanced toward the living room. "How is he today? He was so confused yesterday. The doc's visit threw off his routine." He cocked his head. "Is he being as obstinate as usual about taking his meds?"

Shaun huffed. "You know my dad. I tried telling him we needed to treat his urinary tract infection, but he got into a loop. I persuaded him to take them eventually." He peered at Nathan. "I thought you were getting a haircut this morning. Isn't that what you said when you left here last night?" He added a little butter to the frying pan, then dipped a slice of bread into the egg mixture.

Nathan huffed. "Yeah, well, that didn't work out. I ran out of time."

Shaun placed the bread into the pan, and it sizzled.

"Cyn waved to me as I came up the driveway." That brought a smile. "At least *one* of your neighbors isn't an asshole."

The first time Nathan had visited the house, someone had called the cops. All he'd been doing was walking along the road, but the sight of a Black man in Cape Elizabeth had set curtains twitching. It hadn't taken long for the police officers to show up, and Shaun had done all the talking. Nathan's unblinking stare and tense jaw had told Shaun whatever came out of his mouth might have ended with him being arrested.

Nathan ran his hand over his mass of thick, curly hair, and Shaun chuckled. "Hey, I can always use my clippers. I cut my dad's hair, don't I?"

Nathan's dark brown eyes gleamed. "And the less said about that, the better." He cackled. "I'm not letting you anywhere near my hair." Then he stared. "You know what that stupid woman who works at CVS said?" He stroked his chin. "She asked if I wanted to cover up the gray. I thought, what the hell? There isn't *that* much of it—well, maybe a little more here." He touched his temples with his fingertips. "I think it's kind of distinguished." His gaze met Shaun's. "What do you think?"

Shaun turned the bread. "I say do whatever the hell you want. It's your hair." He glanced at the wall clock.

"What time does the party start?"

He smiled. "It's a sort of come-when-you-like affair."

"Let me just check on Peter." Nathan left the kitchen, and Shaun grabbed plates from the cabinet. He lifted the toast from the pan, and by the time Nathan returned, it was ready. He cut his dad's into small pieces.

Nathan frowned. "You're not having any?"

"I'll eat at the party." He handed Nathan a plate, and then went toward the living room. Nathan stopped him at the door.

"You're not ready yet, are you?" Another gleam in his eyes. "Unless you're going there in your sweats."

"Are you okay to help him eat?" Nathan arched his eyebrows, and Shaun sighed. "Stupid question. I'll go get changed." He handed over his dad's plate, then went into his bedroom where he'd laid out a pair of black jeans and a light blue shirt. He knew some of the others would be in costume, but his heart wasn't in it. As he stepped out of his sweats and into his jeans, he caught the murmur of Nathan's voice.

That guy is a godsend.

He'd hired Nathan in late May, but it felt as if he'd been around for much longer. Nathan was older than his predecessors—in his early forties—and obviously knew his stuff. Shaun watched him sometimes when Nathan and Dad sat together at the table, working on a puzzle. He liked how Nathan didn't crowd him, how he spoke slowly, how he held Dad's hand or rubbed his back when Dad seemed anxious.

Most of all, Shaun liked the fact that he didn't have to worry all the time when he was at work. His dad was in good hands.

Nathan has good hands. They were large, strong-looking hands, but then Nathan *was* strong, able to lift Dad out of his chair if needed, to help him onto the seat in the tub. Dad hadn't blinked an eye the first time they'd met, not that Shaun had expected him to: his parents had raised him to believe all men were equal under the skin. *Mom would've liked him.*

Strike that. Mom would have thought Nathan was sexy. She'd always had a thing for Denzel Washington movies, and Dad had often teased her about it when Shaun was growing up. She'd fan herself whenever he was on screen, and Dad would joke that what she needed was a cold shower. Lord, how she'd blush at that.

I miss her. Shaun's thoughts went to the framed photos covering the walls, half of Dad's table, and the mantel above the fireplace. Having them surrounding his dad was important, but sometimes they were a poignant reminder that he'd already lost one parent, and it wouldn't be long before he lost the other. Shaun knew the score. Stage six could last two-and-a-half years at the most, and many people never made it to stage seven. And while Alzheimer's was quietly devastating his dad's brain, it wouldn't be the disease that would end up killing him—his death would probably be due to any one of several complications.

He gazed at his reflection, unable to miss the bags under his eyes, the lines around them. His twenty-seventh birthday was approaching fast, but right then he felt old before his time.

Maybe a few hours with the guys will help.

Except when those hours had passed, it would be back to his reality of work and care.

Shaun went into the living room, watching once more as Nathan wiped his dad's lips and chin. He glanced up and smiled. "Good toast." Then he joined Shaun in the hallway, and they walked into the kitchen. "Yeah, he's still pretty confused," Nathan said in a low voice. "I'll see if he wants me to read to him while you're gone." He looked Shaun up and down. "Better."

"I suppose I could've rented a costume, or pulled one together, but—"

Nathan shook his head. "You don't need more stuff to think about, you need less." He paused. "These friends you're going to see... Are they the same ones as last time?"

"Yeah."

"And you see them every couple of months or so? Because that seems to be a pattern."

"Not really. It's just the way it's worked out. We went to a party at New Year's, and the next time we saw each other was April for a wedding. Since then, yeah, there's been that birthday party not long after you started working here, a BBQ at the end of August..." Another glance at the clock. "Look, I won't be gone long, just a couple of hours."

Nathan frowned. "This is your first time away from him since August? Man, you need a longer break than that. If you want to stay late, that's okay by me. It's not like you pay me by the hour, right?"

For a moment, Shaun wavered. Levi always set off fireworks at the end of the night, and it had been a while since he'd seen those. Plus, he really hated being the first to leave every time. Then his overactive duty gland took over, and he shook his head. "I can't."

"Sure you can." Nathan's eyes were warm. "Think about it, at least. If you change your mind, call me. And in the meantime, I'm gonna put on one of your dad's favorite DVDs, and we'll watch that. Unless there's a book he'd like me to read."

The probability was Dad wouldn't even know Shaun had gone.

"Thanks for this." He shuddered out a sigh. "I don't know what I'd do without you."

Nathan patted his arm. "This is what I'm here for, isn't it? Now go have a good time."

Shaun went into the living room, stopping beside his dad's chair. "I'll see you later, Dad," he murmured before bending to kiss his forehead.

Dad looked up at him. "You going somewhere? Don't stay out too late. Remember, you have school in the morning."

Shaun straightened and left the room. He lived for those moments when Dad knew him, knew what day it was, but they were becoming infrequent. *He doesn't understand what's happening to him.*

Maybe that was a good thing.

Shaun took a sip of the punch and grimaced. "Wow. It's stronger than usual." He set the glass aside with a shudder. "I think I'll stick to soda." Not that he'd intended drinking more than a mouthful: it was a two-hour round trip, give or take, and he was never one to drink and drive.

Beside him, Dylan chuckled. "*Now* you know why I convinced Mark to come here by taxi." He gestured to the others. "Not many costumes this year. Except for Levi, of course, and Grammy in her witch's hat." He grinned. "That hat has seen better days. She might need a new one for next year. I swear it's the same one she wore when we were in ninth grade."

Shaun wouldn't have known. He'd only met Grammy when he was seventeen. He gazed at Dylan's boyfriend. "So... I have to ask... How long have you known you were bi?"

"A while, I guess. And feel free to ask. Everyone else has."

Shaun chuckled. "Did you expect anything less when you stroll in here with a gorgeous guy on your arm? And he *is* gorgeous. He could be a model." Dylan coughed, and Shaun gave him an inquiring glance. "Something I said?"

"Okay, I might as well tell you, because Seb's not gonna be able to keep quiet for long about *this*." Dylan leaned in. "He's a soon-to-be ex-porn star," he whispered.

Shaun opened his eyes wide. "Kudos, dude. Whoa." Despite the quivering in his stomach that always accompanied any amount of time away from home, he chuckled. "Seb must be jealous as hell."

Dylan rolled his eyes. "He hasn't stopped drooling since we got here. But enough about Mark.

How's your dad?"

He shrugged. "Same shit, different day." Another glance at the clock in the corner. "And maybe I should be getting back."

"You just got here," Dylan remonstrated. "Isn't his nurse with him?"

"Yeah, and he offered to stay longer if I wanted."

Dylan beamed. "Then if he's okay with it, take him up on it. You've been here how long?"

"Two hours and fifteen minutes, but who's counting?" Then there was the travel time. It all added up to more than four hours away from home, and a bad case of the guilts. He sighed. "I can't. It doesn't feel right. I'd be taking advantage of him."

"No," Dylan said gently. "Taking advantage would be if you did this every night. You need a break, dude."

"That's what Nathan said."

"Then Nathan sounds like a wise man. A good man, too."

Shaun smiled. "He is. He's great with Dad. The in-home nurse before him was okay, but I always got the feeling she had someplace else to be, you know? When Nathan's with Dad, I feel as if he gets all Nathan's attention. Not that I get to see that much of him. I walk through the door after work, we chat about Dad's day, and then he leaves." The conversation earlier had been one of the longest they'd shared in the seven months Nathan had worked for him.

"At least you know *he's* not about to announce he's pregnant, like the last one."

Shaun laughed, but then his stomach clenched. "I'm hoping he'll stick around until the end."

Dylan's face tightened. "I keep forgetting. There's no curing this, is there?"

He squared his shoulders. "Nope, it's pretty fucking inevitable. And it's all downhill from here."

Dylan gave him a hug. "I'm gonna repeat my offer. If you need a break, even if it's one night, call me, and I'll book you into the hotel. Okay?"

Shaun returned the hug. "The day you guys let me in was the luckiest day of my life." They'd been his life raft back when he was seventeen and his mother had gotten diagnosed, and he suspected they would be again, before all this was over.

Nathan was another lifeline, one Shaun couldn't imagine being without.

In ways Nathan would never suspect.

Chapter Two

Shaun closed the front door behind him. Nathan sat on the couch, a Kindle in his hand. He glanced up as Shaun took off his coat. "Good party? Your dad went to bed about an hour ago." He set the Kindle aside on the seat cushion.

"The party was great. How was he?"

Nathan smiled. "He was telling me about the time he made those bookcases." He pointed to the side wall covered in bookshelves, framing the large window. "Apparently you helped."

Shaun chuckled. "And just how many times have you heard that story?"

"A few. Gets cuter every time I hear it." He grinned. "Did you really hit your thumb with a hammer?"

"God yes, several times. But I *was* six years old." Shaun glanced at the clock over the fireplace. "It's late. I shouldn't have stayed so long."

"Yes, you should." Nathan's tone was firm. "And I'm not in any hurry to get home. Your shift starts at eleven tomorrow morning, right?"

He nodded.

"Besides, I was hoping we could talk about something."

Shaun's stomach clenched. It was an involuntary reaction that occurred frequently, and always linked to the feeling that he was about to hear bad news. "Is it something that can be discussed over tea?"

Nathan blinked. "At this hour?"

Shaun crooked his finger. "Follow me." He walked through the arch that led to the rear of the house. The white kitchen always reminded him of his mom. Sometimes he could still see her, standing at the blue-painted table, her hands submerged in a bowl of flour as she made pastry. Shaun went over to the cabinet, opened it, and took out the tin that contained his special tea. He removed a box and set it on the countertop.

Nathan picked it up. "Celestial Seasonings Sleepytime Vanilla herbal tea. I've seen this before." He smiled. "The name and the teddy bear in the nightshirt and nightcap always make me think of my grandma. She used to drink this." He cleared his throat. "I wanted to try the peach one. But I wasn't sure how old the tea was. For all I know, it was *your* grandma's tea."

Shaun snorted. "It was Mom's. Well, not *this* box. She used to drink it last thing at night. I got to like it too." Shaun filled the electric kettle. "Of course, when I was a kid, the kettle sat on the stove, and whistled when it came to the boil." He peered at Nathan. "Well? Gonna join me?"

"Do you have peach?"

He smiled. "Sure. I've got peach, honey…" Shaun opened the box and took out a tea bag. "Have a seat." When Nathan did as instructed, Shaun popped the tea bags into two cups. "So… what did you want to talk about?"

Nathan leaned on his elbows, his fingers laced. "Okay, stop me if I'm talking out of turn…I mean, you might have all this already worked out, but…"

Shaun had never known Nathan to be so hesitant. "Worked what out?"

Nathan cocked his head to one side. "Has your dad put anything in place yet? I mean, for when…"

Ah. Shaun got where he was going. "He set up a Durable Power of Attorney for Health Care a few years ago. Having gone through all this with Mom, he wasn't gonna be caught out."

"So you get to make medical decisions for him if and when the time comes that he's no longer able to make his own. Or he's unwilling to."

Shaun nodded.

"But it's something you don't even want to think about, right?" Nathan's eyes were kind.

The kettle beeped, and Shaun poured boiling water into the cups. He brought them over to the table. "You have to let it steep for a while." His stomach was in knots.

Nathan sniffed. "Smells good." He leaned back in his chair. "It's okay, I get it. None of us want to think about losing someone we love, but it's best to be prepared. At least your dad was switched on enough to get it done. Trust me, you don't want to leave it till it's too late."

Shaun gave him a speculative glance. "Why do I get the feeling you're speaking from experience?"

He shrugged. "Because I am? I see it a lot. Most of the people I take care of are getting on in years."

Shaun grasped the paper tag at the end of the string and dunked the tea bag up and down with a gentle motion. "How did you get into nursing?" Whenever he looked at Nathan, one term always came to mind—Gentle giant. He had to be at least six feet tall, which made Shaun's five-feet-seven feel tiny in comparison.

"My momma always says it's my calling." Deep brown eyes focused on Shaun, and he stilled for a moment, aware of Nathan's scrutiny. "But I guess it's because of my grandfather. He had dementia too. Except most of *his* kids weren't as patient with him as you are with your dad."

"What do you mean?"

"If your dad says something that's not right, you don't correct him, because you know that'll only confuse him, right? Well, my aunts and uncles just got irritated with him. My mom, not so much. And whenever I visited, I made sure to sit with him, be aware of his mood, give him a helping hand if he needed one…"

"You're really good with Dad," Shaun acknowledged. "You're so… calm with him."

"Maybe that's because I'm a calm person. And I like taking care of people. Helping them if I can."

"Did you work in a hospital?"

Nathan nodded. "I specialized in geriatrics. And the hospital was okay. I often got asked to do stuff like mop a spill on the floor. As if people didn't know I was a nurse. All our uniforms were color-coded, right? So you can see at a glance who's a doctor, nurse… But it happens. The thing was, I saw so many patients, and there was never enough time to focus on them. That's why I decided to take this route. I get to spend one-on-one time with people." He mimicked Shaun and gently swirled the tea bag around the cup. "Can I ask you something?"

"Sure."

"You said you went through all of this with your mom. When was this?"

Shaun reached for the bowl of sugar and spooned some into his tea. "I was seventeen when she was diagnosed with stage four colon cancer."

"Aw shit." Nathan's face fell. "I'm guessing it wasn't long before she passed."

"Not really, no." There hadn't been enough time to say all the things he'd wanted to. By the time he'd accepted that she was going, she'd gone.

"When did you notice the first signs in your dad?"

"He was diagnosed not long after Mom went, maybe a year, but I think the signs were already visible before she passed. I just thought he was getting forgetful, you know? He couldn't recall names, faces… Then he started repeating himself a lot. He'd misplace stuff, and it would turn up in the oddest places." Shaun sipped his tea, but it was difficult to swallow. "I thought he was coping badly with Mom's death. I didn't think it could be anything else. He was only forty-nine, for Christ's sake."

"I know most people are older when they get diagnosed. But your doc picked up on it. That was a good thing." Nathan cleared his throat. "Something I've been meaning to ask you. Can you put a picture of a toilet on his bathroom door? And maybe leave the light on in there at night. It might help."

Shaun knew what that was about. His dad's incontinence was worsening. But then again, so were a lot of things. His dad's moods, for one. "Some days he seems so… apathetic."

Nathan nodded. "Mood swings are a bitch. He can be sad one minute, then frustrated, anxious… And I know it hurts when he doesn't know you. You have to make the most of those moments when he does."

Shaun's throat tightened. *Yeah.*

Nathan sipped his tea and smiled. "This is good. My mom would love this. She's always telling me to drink less caffeine."

He chuckled. "She's a *mom*. That's what they do."

"And what you said about me being good with your dad? So are you. I know how difficult it can be, watching him become less and less the person you remember. You just gotta love him." Then Nathan reached across the table and gave Shaun's hand a squeeze. "You're doing an awesome job. You work, you take care of him... keeping all those plates spinning takes a lot of energy. Just make sure you keep back a little for yourself."

"I couldn't do this without you." Shaun's face grew hot. "I mean it."

That got his hand another squeeze. "I like Peter. I wish I'd known him before all this. He strikes me as the kind of guy who doesn't give a shit about the color of a person's skin."

Shaun smiled. "You just nailed it. My mom was the same." He let out a wry chuckle. "My mom would've loved you." When Nathan arched his eyebrows, heat surged over Shaun's cheeks. "If I tell you the names of some of her favorite movies, that might explain it. *Training Day, Man On Fire, American Gangster, Philadelphia, Crimson Tide, The Bone Collector...*"

Nathan laughed. "Oh, *I* get it. She had a thing for Denzel, huh? Obviously a woman with good taste." He cocked his head. "And what about you? Do *you* like Mr. Washington?"

"He's okay." Shaun thought Nathan was better-looking. He loved how Nathan's skin was the color of raw honey, deep but golden. Those warm brown eyes didn't miss much. That summer, he'd loved the reddish tone in Nathan's hair that only showed when the sun hit it a certain way. He loved how Nathan's cheekbones popped out every time he smiled. The laughter lines around his eyes…

Denzel has nothing on you.

Then he remembered who Nathan was, and thinking such thoughts felt highly inappropriate.

He freed his hand to grasp his cup. "Something you said… about being asked to mop up spills… Did you have to cope with a lot of that?"

Nathan shrugged. "Maine's a pretty pale state. In fact, I think it's still the whitest state in the nation. So yeah, sometimes I stick out a bit, and there are a *lot* of racist assholes. You'd think some of them had never seen a Black dude. One time I did the math. Figures say 1.38 percent of Maine inhabitants are African American. Do you know how many that is? About eighteen thousand. I ain't so rare."

"Were you born in Maine?"

Nathan shook his head. "Mom was a Southern girl who married a railroad engineer. When my dad got a job with the Maine Northern Railway Company, we moved out here. Dad died before he could retire, and then Mom moved downstate to Augusta. Why she stayed in Maine, I'll never know. She must like it."

"And you moved to Portland."

Nathan's smile reached his eyes. "First time I saw the Atlantic, that was it, a done deal. I fell in love with the ocean, hook, line, and sinker." He bit his lip. "This has to be the most personal conversation we've ever had."

"Then it's long overdue. But we don't get that

much time to talk. You arrive and I go to work, or I come home and you leave."

"I've been meaning to talk to you about that."

Shaun held back a smile. "Something else we need to discuss? This seems to be the night for it."

Nathan wrapped his hands around his cup. "Okay, this is how I see it. You come home, I leave, and suddenly you've swapped one job for another. Now, I know you don't see your dad like that, but I'm right, aren't I? You walk through that front door, and switch from Shaun Clark, server, to Shaun Clark, caregiver. So what I'm suggesting is… a buffer zone."

Shaun frowned. "Huh?"

"Look, the health care company pays my salary, right? You agree on how many hours I work. So… what if… two days a week… when you come home, I *don't* leave right away? What if I work an extra couple of hours? That way, you get a little downtime. You can do your laundry, wash the dishes, shop for groceries, whatever. And the reason I'm saying this?" His expression grew grave. "I know you only work thirty hours, but for the rest of time, you're looking after Peter, and it's taking its toll. Now, there's no one else around here to look out for you—except me." Those warm brown eyes locked on his. "You can't keep this up, Shaun. Something's gonna give, and I don't want it to be your health, mental or otherwise." He held up his hands. "I'm sorry if you feel I'm being too personal, or taking liberties, but I had to say something."

"It's okay," Shaun said quickly. "And… I like your suggestion."

Nathan sagged. "Thank you. I was afraid you'd see it as intruding."

"No. You're very kind. I do think it's imposing

on *you*, however. You'd be losing time."

Nathan laughed. "Trust me, I don't have a lot to occupy my time. There's just me—and my cat."

Shaun smiled. "You have a cat?"

He grinned. "No, I think he has me. I'm pretty sure Cat thinks he's in charge."

Shaun blinked. "'Cat'? How… original."

"When I got him from the Animal Refuge League in Westbrook, they told me Cat was a girl. But when I took her to the vet to get her shots, they asked if I wanted her neutered. I said, 'Don't you mean spayed?' and they said 'No—neutered. Your cat is a boy.'"

"Wasn't it obvious?"

Nathan chuckled. "He was a super hairy tiny kitten. Maybe it was difficult to tell." He glanced at the wall clock. "And speaking of Cat, it's time I went home." He met Shaun's gaze. "You finish work at five tomorrow, don't you?" Shaun nodded. "Well, don't hurry home. Take your time. Go sit on the Eastern Prom and gaze at the ocean. I can highly recommend it. Does wonders for the spirit."

"I may just do that." He let out a sigh. "You're right. I'll talk to the company about changing your hours."

Nathan stood. "Thanks for the tea. I need to put that on my grocery list. I'll see you in the morning. Sleep well."

Shaun stood too. "Thank you. For listening, for thinking of me… All of it."

"You're welcome." Nathan flashed him a familiar smile.

Shaun walked him to the front door, and waved as Nathan drove his car away from the curb. He closed it and locked up.

He'd known the moment he'd met Nathan that he was one of the good guys, and their conversation only served to confirm his assessment.

A very *attractive* good guy.

Chapter Three

November 2

Shaun stuffed his black apron into the hamper by the rear door. His stomach rumbled as a reminder that he'd skipped lunch. He usually grabbed a bite to eat before an eleven o'clock shift, but his morning had been a little hectic.

What made it worse? The look in his dad's eyes as Shaun cleaned him up.

He hates this. He hates what he's becoming. The sorrow and embarrassment evident on his dad's face tore Shaun's heart.

"Hey Shaun," Diane called out from the archway that led into the café. "Someone here to see you."

Shaun took a peek, and smiled when he saw Ben standing there, peering at the counter, and sniffing. Shaun walked over to him. "Hey. What are you doing here?"

"I was in Portland, I thought I'd stop by and say hi."

"Shouldn't you be slaving away behind a cash register?"

Ben rolled his eyes. "I do get a day off, y'know. And I'm in Portland for two reasons. One, Wade's birthday is coming up, and I have no clue what to get that man—other than the obvious."

Shaun had to know. "And what's that?"

Ben's eyes twinkled. "Duh. A big red bow, tied around… something." He glanced at the customers around him and leaned forward in a conspiratorial manner. "I'd say what that something is, but I don't wanna scare off your clients."

"And the second reason?" Ben was a dose of fresh air.

"I had to go to the clinic to get tested. So I thought, seeing as I was here, I'd see what my buddy was doing."

That one word was enough to warm Shaun through. "Your timing is great. I just finished for today."

Ben's face fell. "Oh. Are you going home?"

"No. I was gonna walk down to the water and sit for a while. I have to eat. Wanna join me?"

Ben narrowed his gaze. "What are we eating?"

"It's a surprise."

"Oh no. I'm not agreeing to anything until I know what's going in my mouth."

Shaun grinned. "I didn't think you were that particular about what you put in there. But okay. Belgian fries, cheese curds, duck gravy…" He waited for the explosion.

Ben's eyes widened and his face lit up. "Oh my God. I fucking *love* poutine! Shaun, I love you."

Shaun waved his hand. "Give me a minute to put two takeout boxes together. I'll meet you outside. You're scaring the customers."

Ben cackled and headed out of the door.

Shaun pulled his phone from his pocket and composed a quick text.

Eating with a friend. I won't be too late.

Seconds later, Nathan's reply pinged back. *We're fine here. Peter's asleep in his chair. Enjoy.*

He grabbed a couple of takeout boxes. "Can I have two portions of poutine?"

Sandy, the chef, smiled. "Sure. Give 'em here." He filled the boxes with a heap of fries, then added the cheese curds before ladling duck gravy over the contents. As he secured the takeout, he gave Shaun an inquiring glance. "You okay today, Shaun?"

He pasted on a smile. "I'm fine. See you Thursday."

"Hey, relax a little your days off, all right?" Sandy squeezed Shaun's shoulder. "Take it easy."

Shaun nodded and took the boxes. As an afterthought, he picked up two plastic forks from a tray, and slipped them into his coat pocket. *Can't eat poutine with our fingers.* He said goodbye to the other servers, then walked through the café to where Ben stood on the sidewalk, staring toward the ocean. "Let's walk," Shaun said as he joined him.

"Where are we going?" Ben snuck a peek at the takeout. "Christ, I'm drooling here."

"There's a bench on the Eastern Prom. It's got a great view."

"Sold." Then Ben came to a stop. "Wait a sec. What's to see? It's getting dark already. And it's cold."

Shaun held out a box. "You want poutine? Stop whining and sit with me."

That earned him another eye roll. "Fine. We can sit in the dark and eat. We'll probably get robbed by raccoons."

"It's fairly well-lit. You'll see the raccoons coming." He gave Ben his portion. "Here. Keep your hands warm." They strolled down India Street, the ocean ahead of them. Twilight had already come to an end, and the sky was taking on that velvety hue Shaun loved. When they reached the trail, they turned left, and found an empty bench looking out to sea, nestled between the Ocean Gateway Pier and the Maine State Pier. Boats bobbed on the water, ropes creaked, and waves slapped against the hulls.

Shaun sat, the box in his lap. "Are you okay?"

"Me? I'm doing great."

"It's just that you mentioned a clinic. Tested for what?"

Ben smiled. "HIV, STIs, the works. Wade went too. But I don't expect they'll find anything, because I haven't been with anyone and neither has he. We're just testing to make sure. I don't think that's a bad habit to get into, do you?" His smile morphed into a grin. "Saves us a small fortune not having to buy condoms."

"I'm glad you said that while I wasn't eating."

Ben snickered. "Damn. I'll have to do better." They opened their boxes and the aroma was heavenly. Ben let out a happy sigh. "The only way you could improve on this? A box of Cheez-Its to dip in the gravy."

"I'll tell the chef to add it to the menu. I'm pretty sure he'll say no, because… Ew." Shaun popped a couple of gravy-and-cheese curd-covered fries into his mouth. Delicious. For a few minutes there was silence as they ate, broken only by Ben's appreciative noises.

His hunger abated, Shaun seized his courage. "I *am* kinda surprised to see you."

Ben frowned. "Why would you be?"

He shrugged. "I guess because we haven't been all that close. Not that I'm blaming you for that," he added quickly. "But I've always felt as if I was on the outside looking in with you guys. A lot of that was down to me."

Ben said nothing for a moment, and Shaun's stomach was in knots. Ben set his empty box on the seat, and leaned forward, elbows on his knees. "You've always been quiet. Private. We didn't like to pry."

"I will always be grateful to you. You pulled me into your group at a time when I really needed it."

Ben squeezed his knee. "Dude… It was a shit time. We couldn't offer any help. All we could do was be there for you."

"Hey, the support you gave? That was awesome. I think all of you were my escape from reality. But ever since then, I guess I feel as if I've been hanging around on the edge. Not that I'm complaining. I'm grateful I don't get the same grilling the others get."

Ben grinned. "I can soon change that. Do you *want* me to start grilling you?" He leaned back against the bench. "I know we laugh and joke a lot, and yank each other's chains all the time, but we do know when to be respectful. I guess we pulled back too much. Maybe we need to find some middle ground."

Shaun gazed at the ocean. "If I'm honest, I built a wall between me and you. Not just you—all of you. Whenever I was with you, I put the private side of my life on hold. I had two worlds and I kept them separate. But you guys got me through Mom's death, and like I said, I will always be grateful."

"Have you any idea how hard it's been, keeping my mouth on a leash?"

Shaun chuckled. "I can imagine."

"*So* many times I've wanted to ask you what was going on in your life, but I got the feeling you were struggling, so I backed off. I was *dying* to ask if you had a girlfriend... Or a boyfriend..."

Shaun laughed. "Of course you were. Honestly, why should it be such a big deal to know if someone is gay, straight, whatever?" He was surprised the topic hadn't come up before now. *Maybe they assumed if I was anything other than straight, I'd have said so.*

Yeah, they didn't know him as well as they thought.

"It isn't a big deal," Ben assured him. "Who gives a shit about labels? We don't. I mean that. We don't give a shit—unless you're into wild and crazy things, you know, like goats. Other than that, we don't care."

He chuckled. "But you still wanna know whether I'm into girls or boys, don't you? You can't help yourself."

Ben's eyes widened. "Of course. How can I set you up with someone if I don't know who to set you up with?" He paused for a moment. "You said you felt as if you were on the outside looking in. It's okay to keep stuff to yourself, all right? It's where you've drawn a line, and we won't cross it. Even though we've known you for what, nearly ten years? If you don't think you're ready to share stuff on that level, it's okay. Take your time." Another pause. "For all *I* know, you might be interested in boys, girls, both, neither, a specific person..."

Shaun shook his head. "Like I said, you can't help yourself." He pasted on a serious expression. "So you're saying I should keep my love affair with goats to myself?" Ben choked, and he laughed. "Damn. And you'd finished eating too." Then Shaun sighed heavily. "There isn't anyone in my life, of course. Right about when I was starting to get interested, Mom got her diagnosis. Nothing puts things into perspective like learning your mom is about to die. And when she'd gone, suddenly there was Dad to deal with. So I don't talk about my love life because I don't have one." After a moment's hesitation, he added, "I've never had one."

Ben gave an exaggerated swallow. "Dude. Are you telling me what I *think* you're telling me?"

Shaun rolled his eyes. "Yes, Ben. I'm a virgin."

He blinked. "A twenty-six-year-old virgin. Oh. Em. Gee." Then he smiled. "News flash for ya. You're not as rare as you think." Before Shaun could question further on that, Ben continued. "I do get it. You had so much on your mind, romance took a back seat. Totally understandable." His eyes sparkled. "Man, we need to get your cherry popped."

"No, *we* don't. Remember that line you said you wouldn't cross? You just did." He'd known Ben couldn't resist, and maybe deep down, Shaun had wanted to be on the receiving end of the same kind of treatment all the others got.

Maybe I've had enough of being on the outside. Maybe I want in.

"I'm sorry," he said quietly. "That came out way harsher than I'd intended."

"When it comes to you, I make allowances. None of us has any fucking *clue* what your life is like, okay?" A pause. "But now that we're finally talking... There's something I've been meaning to ask you for a while now."

"Ask. I might even answer."

Ben inclined his head in the direction of Middle Street where DuckFat was located. "You're a server in a café. How could you afford a nurse to take care of your dad?"

"Because my wages as a server don't pay for that. Dad has Nathan because of Mom's insurance, Dad's critical illness benefits, and every other benefit he paid into. So if you want to know someone else I'm profoundly grateful to? It's people like Joel. All those financial advisers who made sure I was provided for. There's no mortgage on the house. The bills get paid. And so does Nathan."

Ben sighed. "I think this conversation was long overdue."

Shaun couldn't agree more. "At Aaron's BBQ, I did something I rarely do—I opened up to someone. Maybe that was the first step. I never talk about Dad. It just… hurts. But I'm enough of a realist to know I'm going to need my friends. The end, as they say, is in sight."

Ben's breath caught. "How long do you think he's got?"

"It could be a couple of years, it could be less than that. There's no way of knowing." He stared at the box in his lap. "He's turning sixty in December. Hopefully, he'll make it that far."

"You ever need to talk, you know where I am, all right? Camden is *not* at the fucking end of the earth, okay? If you call, I'll come." Ben's face was solemn. "Swear to God, I'll be there for you."

Shaun swallowed hard, and tears pricked his eyes. "Thank you." He sniffed.

"I just wish you weren't alone in all this. You need someone to lean on."

Nathan's face was right there in his head. "I've got someone." When Ben stilled, Shaun held up his hand. "It's nothing like that, okay? They're just a friend. I don't think they can be more than that." The caution with pronouns felt outdated, considering their conversation.

"But you're attracted to them?" Ben locked gazes with him.

Shaun took a huge step out of his comfort zone. "Yes, I am. He's… he's special."

Ben expelled a long breath. "Thanks for trusting me. I won't breathe a word. But I *will* hope."

Shaun smiled. "You do that. I'll hope too."

He was deluding himself and he knew it. But right from the day they'd met, there'd been something about Nathan. Shaun really liked him, and it felt as if Nathan liked him too. God, he'd almost heard the *click*. But Nathan was a professional, and that was one line Shaun wouldn't cross.

He could dream, however. Those nights when he lay in the dark, letting his imagination run riot, picturing himself wrapped in a pair of strong arms… He'd feel guilty as hell when he woke, but at the same time he'd yearn to go back to sleep, to pick up where the dream left off.

He *clung* to those dreams.

Shaun cleared his throat. "I'd better go. Nathan needs to get home too." He stood, and Ben joined him. Shaun grabbed the empty boxes and stuffed them into the nearby trash can. To his surprise, Ben gave him a hug.

"You're not on the outside anymore, okay? I'm officially pulling you in and we're *keeping* you in." He released Shaun. "But when it comes to you, I'll ease up on the chain-yanking. No one needs to know more than you're prepared to share, all right?"

Shaun felt a little lighter. "Thank you. Now, are you done, or do you still have a birthday gift to find?"

Ben grinned. "I'm off now to find a big red bow."

Shaun laughed. "I'm sure Wade will have a lot of fun unwrapping you—I mean, it." He shivered. "I'm gonna go home. It's getting cold."

"What do you mean, 'getting'? My nuts froze half an hour ago." Ben waved as he headed toward the parking lot.

Shaun walked briskly to the garage on Fore Street. Meeting Ben had provided a much-needed break, but now it was time to face reality.

Time to go home.

Chapter Four

Nathan headed for the hot shower that had been calling him for the past couple of hours. He had two days to himself, and a list of stuff to do that was twice that long. He'd gotten used to not working Tuesdays and Wednesdays, but it meant his weekend had moved too.

As he undressed in his bedroom, he smiled. *Shaun took my advice.* Shaun's text had taken him by surprise, but Nathan had been delighted. And when Shaun had walked through the front door, he'd appeared relaxed. Meeting up with his friend had obviously done a lot of good.

He's such a sweet guy. It pained Nathan to see Shaun with his dad, especially those moments when Peter gave him a blank stare as if Shaun were a stranger. All Nathan wanted to do was draw Shaun to him and hold him, cradle him in his arms, and comfort him. There was something about Shaun that called to him. His soft brown hair, soulful brown eyes, full lips, the dark beard that hugged his jawline… all of it added up to a gorgeous man who made Nathan's heart beat that little bit faster. Forcing himself not to think of Shaun like that was probably the most difficult task of Nathan's day. Once he was out of there, he allowed his thoughts to drift. There were times, however, when he sat with Peter, quiet times interrupted only by the ticking of the clock above the fireplace, when Nathan longed to tell him what a beautiful son he'd raised.

His lips remained sealed. There were some lines that could not be crossed.

When his phone burst into life with smooth, synthesized tones, Nathan picked it up. Jadyn's face filled his screen, the photo Phoebe had taken of him at Christmas a couple of years ago. On top of Jadyn's head was a bright red Santa hat, and he was grinning like a loon. It was the perfect picture of his brother: Jadyn was a Christmas *nut*.

Nathan clicked on Answer. "Hey bro. Been a while since you called. Have you put up your Christmas lights yet?"

Jadyn snorted. "You think I'd be talking to you if I had? Della would've put me in the hospital in a heartbeat. You *know* the rules, man. Nothing Christmas-y until December first." He clicked his tongue. "Guess there were some questions I should've asked her before I popped the question. Because maybe if I'd known about her rules, things might've been different."

Nathan knew he wasn't serious. "So motherhood hasn't mellowed her yet?"

"Man, you have *no* idea."

"And how is my niece? Living up to her name?" Angel had been born a month ago.

Jadyn sighed happily. "Yeah, 'cause she *is* an angel. Momma's been here for a week, and she doesn't want to let go of her first granddaughter. Which is kinda why I'm calling."

"Anything wrong?"

"This is just a heads up. I'm getting signals from Momma."

"What kind of signals?"

"Well, now that we've given her two grandkids, and Phoebe's given her one, she's got a taste for it. You *know* how her mind works, dude. *I'm* settled, Phoebe's settled, so that just leaves you. Add to that the fact that she's retired now, and I think we can safely say you're her next project."

What the fuck? "And what exactly makes you say that?"

"She's been making noises lately. Kind of Nathan-needs-to-find-himself-a-girl noises. Nathan-needs-to-settle-down noises. 'Nathan ain't getting any younger.' You getting the picture?"

All too clearly. *Aw shit.*

"Don't you think it's time you told her?"

What the— "Told her what?"

"Oh, come *on*. *Momma* might not have noticed who your pinups were when you were growing up, but *I* sure did. She probably thought you were *really* into musical theater. And when you think about it, wasn't that a big enough clue?"

There seemed little point denying it. "You know, I figured I might never have to tell her. I've got to the age of forty-three and she *still* doesn't know." Except deep down, he knew it was inevitable.

"Ya think? Since when has anything gotten past her? Trust me, she knows you're gay. Hell, *I* know you're gay, and I'm *definitely* not the sharpest knife in the drawer. So I think she's just waiting on you to say something. What puzzles me is why you think it'd be such a big deal for her. She's one of the most liberal-minded people I've ever known. It wouldn't bother her none."

"You said it yourself. Grandkids. Think about it. When Della announced she was pregnant with Joe, I thought Momma was gonna broadcast it in every newspaper in the state. I tell her I'm gay, and all she'll see is a *huge* sign over my head saying *No kids from this one.*"

"There's this newfangled idea. Maybe you've heard of it. It might have made it to coastal Maine. It's called *adoption*. There's another one as well, surrogacy. I hear they're catchin' on."

"Yeah. Funny man."

"Tell her. She's not gonna explode."

"Yeah, you *say* that."

"Man, she knows, I'm telling you. And if she does, then she's already gotten used to the idea that there won't be any teeny tiny Nathanettes running around."

"'Nathanettes'? Where do you get your ideas?"

"Make the call, please? Then maybe we can *all* have a relaxed Christmas this year." He paused. "You *are* gonna visit her for Christmas, aren't you? You're already in the doghouse because you haven't been up here lately."

"Yeah, yeah, I'll visit. And thanks for the warning. Kiss Angel and Joey for me."

"I'll kiss Angel, 'cause she smells beautiful. Joey smells like every two-year-old boy I've ever encountered, so no *way* am I kissing that."

Nathan laughed. Jadyn adored his kids.

"Hey, before I let you go…" Jadyn paused again. "Are you coming home for Thanksgiving?"

He hadn't even thought about it. "Not sure right this second. I'll let you know, okay?" Hell, it was only November second. He had *weeks* to decide.

Jadyn whistled. "Man, I wouldn't like to be in your shoes at Christmas if you don't. Momma will be taking a piece off of *you*, instead of the turkey, or the ham, or whatever else she's planning on serving up." He chuckled. "And she can do it too. She's still got Daddy's electric carving knife. So bear that in mind?" He said goodbye and disconnected.

Nathan tossed his phone onto the bed, then walked into the bathroom. Momma had laid not-so-subtle hints about seeing where he was living. Augusta wasn't that far away, but until recently she'd had too much on her plate to allow her time to visit. Plus, his schedule didn't make it easy. But that summer she'd retired, and Nathan knew it wouldn't be long before the hints started up again.

I'll deal with those when they happen.

He turned on the shower and climbed into the tiny enclosure. The whole apartment was a little on the small side, but he didn't need a lot of space, not when it was just him.

And that was what lay at the heart of it. Nathan was getting tired of being alone.

Nathan poured hot soup into a bowl, carried it carefully into his living room, and sat at the table in the corner. He took a bite of the grilled cheese sandwich he'd already placed there, but before he'd swallowed it, his phone rang again.

He sighed when he saw Momma's name. *Guess Jadyn was right.* He clicked on Answer. "Hey Momma.

How are you??

"Don't you 'hey Momma' me. I haven't seen you for months."

Dear Lord, she sounded pissed.

"I have a job, Momma."

"So does Jadyn. So does Phoebe. They still manage to visit me. So if Mohammed won't come to the mountain…"

Oh God. He did *not* like the sound of that. "You want me to visit? Let me find a nurse who can take over from me for a couple of days, then I'll come visit." If it would keep her sweet until Christmas, it would be worth it.

"Who are you taking care of at the moment?"

"A guy in his late fifties with Alzheimer's. But I don't think I'll be working with him for much longer." Nathan didn't want to think about that. It would hurt him to lose Peter, like it hurt him every time he lost a patient, but with Peter, there was also the pain of saying goodbye to Shaun.

Just over five months since he'd started working there, and he couldn't imagine not seeing Shaun's sweet face.

"That's pretty young, isn't it? How sad. Does he have kids?"

"He has a son. And this is gonna hit him hard. His dad is all he has left." Nathan had no idea if there were more relatives in Shaun's life. *Maybe that's something else we should talk about. He's going to need a support network.*

"You're a good man," she said in a softer voice. "That's why you make such a good nurse. You have a lot of empathy. So… don't change your patient's routine just for me. It's not good to do that. It only upsets them."

That was why he loved her so much. "And you're a good, unselfish woman."

She huffed. "I can wait till Christmas... or Thanksgiving?"

The slight inflection was a hint, and he knew it. "I haven't scheduled that far ahead."

She tut-tutted. "You know what they say about all work and no play."

"I know, Momma."

She paused for a moment, and Nathan steeled himself. "You know what? It's not good to be on your own. You're forty-three. Don't you think it's time you settled down? Started a family? If you wait much longer, by the time your kids are born, you'll be ancient."

"Who says I even want kids?"

She let out a loud gasp. "Cross that out. Don't even joke."

"Okay, I'm yanking your chain. I'd love to have kids. But... Momma... There's something I'd been meaning to tell you. For a while now."

"Am I gonna like this?"

It wasn't the best way, over the phone, but he'd gotten this far. "Well, let's see. I... I'm gay."

The silence that followed made his heart sink. *Jadyn was wrong. She didn't have a clue.*

"It took you long enough."

He pulled the phone away from his ear and stared at her photo as if he expected it to come to life and start moving.

"Nathan?"

He hit the speaker icon. "You knew?"

She chuckled. "Did you *hear* me mention the word girlfriend when I said you needed to settle down and start a family? Hmm? So what if you like boys? You can still adopt, right? I know, there are other avenues too, but when I looked them up, I read something about a turkey baster, and that was it, I was outta there."

He tried not to laugh. His momma was amazing.

"But something I gotta say here… You've already got two strikes against you—you're Black, and you live in lily-white Maine. You gotta add being *gay* to that?"

"Momma… It's not as if two of those were a choice."

That earned him another huff. "Is it too much to hope you've got some nice Black boy in your sights? I don't care how old he is, what he looks like—okay, strike that last part. If we need to put a paper bag over his head at family celebrations because he's ugly as sin, maybe *you* need to rethink. You have to consider the genes."

She did not *just say that.*

Momma chuckled. "Now I'm yanking *your* chain. How does it feel?"

"You're incorrigible."

"And you haven't answered my question. Is there someone? Would I like him?"

There was no way he was about to tell her that the only man to attract his attention was a guy in his mid-to-late twenties, with skin the color of peaches and cream.

Then he realized she'd gone quiet. Where Momma was concerned, that was not a good sign.

"You know how your grandma used to tell people how I… knew things before they happened? How she figured she'd named me right? Because I'm having a premonition right now."

He snorted. "Momma, your name might be Cassandra, but that is the *only* similarity between you and some mythical Ancient Greek priestess who could see the future, no matter how badly you'd like it to be true. And before you ask how I know about such things, *you* told me. You told *all* of us kids, many, many times, usually when you were giving us dire warnings of what would happen if we didn't do what you said."

"Don't you try and wriggle out of this. You've got your eye on some white boy, haven't you? Boy, do you have a death wish or something? Folks see you dating a white guy, and they're gonna arm themselves with pitchforks, torches, and rifles."

"Momma? Stop exaggerating and calm down. I am not dating *anyone*, okay? And even if I *was* dating a white guy, the world would not come to an end. And you'd grow to love him. Because can you see me falling in love with anyone who is *not* a beautiful human being, inside *and* out?"

Another bout of silence.

"You know I'm right, don't you, *Sister Rose*?"

"You wouldn't be smart-mouthing your momma now, would you?"

"Wouldn't dream of it. And I mean it. I'll think about Thanksgiving. But right now I *really* need to eat."

"I'll let you go. But you're gonna call me, right?"

"I will, I promise."

"Then go eat." She paused. "There. Doesn't that feel better now it's out in the open? Can't think why you haven't told me until now."

He resisted the urge to snort. "Bye, Momma. We'll talk soon." He disconnected, then attacked his soup and rapidly cooling sandwich. She was right, of course. It did feel better.

He tried not to think about Shaun. What was the point of torturing himself with thoughts of someone he couldn't have? Maybe he had a touch of his momma's gift because he could see Shaun's future, plain as day. His dad would pass, Shaun would grieve, and then he'd start living again. He'd find some sweet girl, settle down, and raise some kids.

Okay, so he was making assumptions, but he'd seen nothing to tell him Shaun's life would be anything other than straight—no matter how badly Nathan might wish things could be different.

Chapter Five

November 5

Nathan helped Peter back to his recliner. "You okay now?"

"No, I'm *not* okay. I can't seem to walk five steps these days without stumbling." He pulled away from Nathan's hand. "You can let go now. Can't exactly fall out of my chair, now can I?" The frustration in his voice was all too evident.

"Anytime you feel unsteady on your feet, you just holler, all right?" Peter had fallen against the wall on his way back from the bathroom. Fortunately, Nathan had been close by. "I can't tell you how many times I've fallen down on my ass. If you saw me dance, you'd understand. All that *rhythm* we're supposed to have? I guess I wasn't in the right line when it was handed out, 'cause I ended up with two left feet, my momma says." It wasn't true, but all Nathan wanted to do was raise a smile.

Peter laughed, and the tension dissipated. "I think maybe I got all yours, then. Laura and I used to go dancing when we were younger. She used to tell me I was a great dancer. Mind you, she was so graceful." He picked up a framed photo from the table beside him, and gazed at it.

Nathan smiled. Peter often mentioned their dancing days, only now and again he got stuck in a loop, and Nathan would do his best to divert him out of it with another topic of conversation. "She was very pretty." Shaun had her eyes, soft and brown and unguarded.

"She was." Peter's Adam's apple bobbed.

Nathan poured him a glass of water from the jug on the table. "Here. You're not drinking enough today."

"Is Shaun at work?" Peter drank a little, then replaced the glass on its coaster.

Nathan shook his head. "He's doing laundry. He won't be long." Peter looked tired. "Why don't you use this all singin' 'n' dancin' chair, and close your eyes for a while? A nap before supper won't hurt."

He nodded. "I might just do that." Peter picked up the remote and pressed a button. His head slowly went back, and Nathan placed a cushion under it. "That feels good," Peter admitted. "Will you still be here when I wake up?"

"Probably not, but I'll see you in the morning."

"'Kay." Peter closed his eyes, and it wasn't long before his breathing changed, becoming deeper. Nathan waited a while, gazing at him. It had been a good day, right up until Peter's little spill. He'd talked a lot, more than usual in fact, and most of the time he'd been lucid. But Nathan had seen too many patients like Peter. Days like this were a blip—reality was a string of days when he spoke more slowly, struggling to put more than three sentences together.

And there are more of those days on the horizon.

He walked quietly out of the living room into the kitchen.

Shaun stood at the table, folding the clean clothes. He glanced at Nathan. "Is he okay?"

"Yeah. Thanks for not crowding him. It was just a little wobble, that's all. Nothing I couldn't cope with."

"Does he do that a lot?"

Nathan didn't believe in sugarcoating facts. It wasn't fair on relatives. "It's getting more frequent."

Shaun's face tightened. "Does that mean—"

"It's one of those things that occurs more and more, the closer we get to the finish line, yes, but it doesn't mean that line is right around the corner," Nathan assured him gently. "I wish I could give you an idea of how long he's got left, but you know everything that I do about the various stages." He'd seen some patients spend two years in Peter's present state, but there had been others who hadn't lasted half that time.

Shaun knew the score. Nathan had seen to that.

He thought back to his conversation with momma, and realized there was something he'd meant to bring up. "You think you can stop folding for a sec, so we can talk?"

"I was just about to grab a bottle of iced tea from the fridge. Want one?"

"Sure." Nathan pulled out a chair and sat while Shaun lifted the laundry basket and set it on the floor. He went to the fridge and returned with two bottles.

"You got something specific you wanna talk about?"

Nathan inclined his head toward the arch. "All those photos of your dad's... I see pictures of you, your parents, but no one else. What about aunts, uncles, cousins, grandparents?"

Shaun opened his bottle and took a long drink. "Both sets of grandparents are gone. Which kinda makes me think with *my* genes, I'm not gonna live to a ripe old age. Both Mom and Dad were an only child. So it's just me." He frowned. "Why do you ask?"

"I got to thinking a few days ago, about who will be there for you when…" He wanted to say *when the time comes*, but he knew Shaun was quick enough on the draw to work that out.

Shaun smiled. "Thanks for thinking of me, but you don't need to worry. I've got my support network all ready to go."

"You mean your friends, right?" When Shaun nodded, Nathan leaned back. "Tell me about them."

"I'd seen most of them going through high school, like you do, but only to nod to. I mean, by the time I reached seventeen, I wasn't friends with any of them. And then everything changed."

"What happened?" Then he realized he already knew. "Ah. Your mom got diagnosed."

Shaun took another drink. "Yeah. I was in the cafeteria, trying to eat my lunch and failing miserably. I'd wanted to stay home with her, but she wouldn't hear of it. She said there was nothing I could do for her, and that my education was more important. So there I was, sitting alone at a table, doing my best to swallow, only there was a rock in my throat. That's how it felt, at any rate. And then this guy from my English class walked over and asked if he could join me. That was Levi." Shaun smiled. "He was the kind of student who gave these quiet, thoughtful answers in class, ones that really made you think. Anyhow, he sat facing me, and we talked, about movies, mostly. He'd gone to see a movie called *Never Let Me Go*, and said it had been awesome. I thought he'd ask a lot of questions, but he didn't. When lunchtime was over, he got up and thanked me." He smiled. "The next day he was back, only this time he wasn't alone."

"Who'd he bring with him?" Nathan liked the sound of Levi.

"Seb. Now, this is where I tell you Seb and Levi are nothing alike. Levi could blend into the background and you'd never know he was there. Seb? Now *there* was a guy with absolutely no filters. You know in all those movies about high school, there's always one kid who's out and proud? That was Seb. He didn't give a shit if students knew he was gay. And then I found out Levi was gay too." Shaun chuckled. "I remember asking if they were dating each other. They both choked laughing."

Nathan smiled. "I'm guessing that was a no." What he liked most about Shaun's revelations was the fact that he was comfortable around gay guys. Nathan had encountered his fair share of homophobic assholes in high school.

"Levi and Seb ate lunch with me from then on, and I liked that. Except little by little, more of Levi's friends joined us. I got the feeling he'd arranged it like that, to trickle them in until I was comfortable with them." Shaun bit his lip. "When I met Finn, I gotta say, I started thinking the universe was trying to tell me something. Because Finn was gay too."

"Three of them are gay?"

Shaun nodded. "It was a relief when Aaron, Dylan, Noah, and Ben showed up, because they were straight." He snorted. "Yeah. I got that wrong, but then so did everyone else. Ben finally came out as gay a while back, Noah's told us he's asexual, and Dylan came to the Halloween party with a friend who turned out to be his boyfriend *and* a porn star. *Then* Dylan tells us he's bi."

Nathan laughed. "They sound like an awesome bunch."

"They are. The stuff they got up to, those last two years of high school…"

"Like what?"

"Like the time Seb got into the IT suite and flipped all the display screens upside down. Then there was the time we all started getting fun facts about cats on our phones."

"He's the prankster, huh?"

"Yeah, but he's not the only one. Someone got Finn really pissed, so he stuck a straw into a packet of yellow mustard, then squeezed the packet into the guy's can of soda when he wasn't looking. And Ben was forever leaving fake poop *everywhere* on April Fool's day."

"They all knew about your mom?"

Shaun nodded. "They were… amazing. They didn't ask a load of questions, but they let me know in little ways that they were there for me. I wasn't alone anymore. And yeah, they know about Dad too."

"Sounds like you have a great network." Nathan smiled. "You're lucky. I'd have given anything to have friends like that in high school."

"Where did you go to school?"

"Houlton High School in upstate Maine. I stuck out a little. There were less than four hundred students, and me and my brother Jadyn were only two of six Black students. He's two years younger than me. We hung out a lot together in high school."

"Are there more of you?"

"There's my sister, Phoebe. She's the youngest." Nathan removed his phone from his pocket and scrolled through his gallery. "Here. That's Jadyn." He held it up for Shaun to see.

Shaun smiled. "He's got a great smile."

"That smile is never far from his face, believe me." Nathan scrolled again. "And this is him with his wife Della, their little boy Joey, and their new baby, Angel."

Shaun grinned. "Aw, those kids are adorable. Do you see much of them?"

"Not as much as their dad would like. And if I don't turn up at Christmas, he might disown me." He scrolled. "This is Phoebe and her partner Leo. They have a little boy, Kelsey." He held out his phone again.

Shaun took it and gazed at the image. "Is that your mom in the background?"

"Yeah."

"She looks nice."

"She may look like butter wouldn't melt, but it's all an act, trust me. Momma rules."

Shaun handed him the phone. "You have a great-looking family." He drank some more. "Actually, there was something I meant to talk to *you* about."

"Oh?"

"This arrangement of yours… where you work a couple of hours longer two days a week…I've thought on it since and… I should've said no when you first suggested it."

"Why?" Nathan couldn't see what the problem was.

"I'm intruding into your time. I know you said it wasn't an imposition, but… You have a life too, right?"

Nathan waved his hand. "Hey, there's just me and Cat, remember?" Shaun's honesty about his friends emboldened him. "Okay, so there *have* been people in my life, but right now, I… I don't have a boyfriend."

He had no idea why his heartbeat quickened. Shaun wasn't going to have a problem with it.

Shaun blinked. "You have *got* to be kidding."

Nathan chuckled. "Yeah. I'm sitting here, listening to you talk about your gay friends, and all the while I'm thinking… What *is* this guy, a fagnet?"

Shaun almost choked on his tea. "A what?"

Nathan bit back a smile. "Okay, maybe I should've come up with a better term. How about… gay flypaper? That works too, 'cause you just pull us in, don't you?"

Shaun shook with laughter. "I haven't got over fagnet yet. How can something so offensive be so funny?"

The sound was infectious, and pretty soon Nathan was laughing too. "I know, right?"

Then Shaun sighed. "I guess you have to go now."

"Yeah. If I get home too late, Cat will poop in my sneakers."

Shaun widened his eyes. "He doesn't do that—does he?"

Nathan laughed again. "No, he'll just ignore me all night—until he wants something."

"Would… would Cat be okay on his own for an evening if you fed him first?"

Shaun's hesitant tone intrigued him. "Why do you ask?"

"Well, I was thinking maybe this Saturday… you could go home to feed him… then come back here and eat with me and Dad." Before Nathan could react, Shaun blurted out, "You know what? Forget I asked. You spend five days a week here. You need a break from us."

"Hey," Nathan said softly. "Do you wanna know how often someone asks me to eat with them? Never. I'd really like that." He cocked his head. "Is this where I should ask if you can cook?"

Shaun's mock gasp of horror was a delight. "Hey."

"I had to ask, right? But your dad's made it this far, so I guess you must be okay." He loved the idea, but he didn't want to impose. Then he smiled. *Just say yes. You know you want to.* "I'd love it. I'm a regular omnivore, so don't worry about serving up something I won't eat. Can I bring something?"

"Just you. If you're sure... I mean, I don't wanna be responsible for Cat sticking his claws in your leg as revenge."

Nathan laughed. "I'll make sure he has plenty of food. I might have to buy him a new toy to sweeten the deal though." He got up. "Thanks for giving me something to look forward to."

"Thanks for saying yes. Of course, I might cheat and order a pizza."

Nathan grinned. "Okay, now you really do have me looking forward to Saturday." He walked to the back door where he'd hung his coat and scarf. "Thanks for the iced tea—and the conversation." He'd gotten to know Shaun a whole lot better, and he liked what he'd heard. Shaun's invitation had come out of the blue, but Nathan figured he just needed some company.

I can be that.

K.C. WELLS

Chapter Six

November 7

"Shaun? Have you seen my glasses?"

Shaun went into the living room and smiled. "Try on top of your head."

His dad reached up slowly, touched the frames, and rolled his eyes. "Christ." He glanced at Shaun. "Is it December yet?"

"No, Dad, it's November seventh." Not knowing the date was becoming a common occurrence. What worried Shaun more was his dad's speech: it seemed almost sluggish.

Dad frowned. "You sure?"

"Yeah, I'm sure. Now, what do you want to read?"

He gave Shaun a puzzled glance. "Who says I want to?"

Shaun pasted on another smile. "You were searching for your reading glasses." Some days his dad appeared more alert, his eyes brighter, and his wit just that little bit quicker.

This was not one of those days.

"Oh. Right." He peered at the bookshelves. "Are those my books?"

"Most of them. How about I bring you one of your favorites?" Shaun was glad his dad still liked to read. It was one of what the doctor had called *preserved skills*. With all the changes going on in his brain, his dad still loved listening to music, telling his stories…

Recently, Shaun had gotten him into audio books, and watching his dad's face as he listened to Andy Serkis narrate *Lord of the Rings* brought Shaun so much peace. In those moments he could forget reality, and pretend.

Until those calm moments crashed and burned, and real life intruded with yet another reminder that it sucked donkey balls.

Dad pointed to his Kindle and earbuds. "Gimme those. I'll listen instead."

"Sure." Shaun handed them to him. "Nathan went home to change, but he's coming back soon to have supper with us."

"Nathan?"

"Your nurse," Shaun explained for the third time that evening. "He was here today, remember?"

"Oh. Oh yeah." Dad smiled. "He's a good boy."

He laughed. "He's not a boy, Dad. He's in his forties."

"Seriously? He looks younger. And at my age, I can call him a boy."

"I'm glad you like him." The fact that he could recall how Nathan looked was a bright spot in Shaun's increasingly cloudy day.

Dad beamed. "He's a hell of a lot better than… the last one. She had… a face only radio… could love." The words came out slow and halting, but the twinkle in his eye eased the tension in Shaun's shoulders.

"Dad!" Shaun was aghast. "You can't say things like that about people."

"Why not? I didn't say it to her, did I?" His face fell. "I didn't—did I?"

"No, of course you didn't," Shaun hastened to assure him. At least, he hoped not. He figured she'd have mentioned something like that.

"Have you seen my glasses?"

Gently, Shaun removed them from his dad's head, folded in the arms, and placed them in the glasses case on the table. "You don't need them if you're listening to a book, right? And now you know where they are for when you do need them."

Dad caught his arm, and gazed into his eyes. "You're a good boy too." His voice was warm.

Shaun bent down and kissed his cheek. "Love you, Dad."

Dad settled back in his chair. "Now shoo so I can listen."

Shaun chuckled and left him to it. He had supper to prepare.

Once inside the kitchen, he let the mask fall and leaned against the countertop, heavy in heart and soul. *He's slipping away from me, little by little.* His decline was more visible in recent weeks, and Shaun struggled to hold on tight to his emotions. The toughest part was not revealing how deeply the changes in his dad affected him.

He pushed his melancholia aside. Nathan would be back soon, and while Shaun felt comfortable around him, he wasn't sure he wanted to bare his soul.

No sooner had he gotten all the ingredients ready when he heard footsteps coming to the back door. He hurried to open it, and Nathan stepped into the warm kitchen, holding a bottle. "I know I'm early. I hope you don't mind." He shivered. "It's getting colder out there."

Relief flooded through him. It was as if Nathan had sensed how badly Shaun needed company. "Of course I don't mind. You're gonna be bored out of your skull watching me cook, though."

Nathan widened his eyes. "No pizza?"

"I changed my mind. Thought I'd make something Mom taught me when I was a teenager." He glanced at Nathan's hand.

"I know you said don't bring anything, but my momma raised me better than that." He held out the bottle. "Hope white wine goes with whatever it is you're cooking."

"Thank you. White wine makes plain old mac and cheese sound more… sophisticated."

Nathan groaned. "You're making mac and cheese?"

Shaun had the feeling he'd chosen well. "Put the wine in the fridge, take off your coat and hang it up, then sit. We can talk while I work."

"Can I go say hello to Peter?"

Shaun shook his head. "He's listening to an audio book. He's in his own little world. You'll see him at supper."

Nathan closed the fridge door, then removed his coat. "Is everything okay?"

"Why'd you ask?"

He shrugged. "Just a feeling. You seem a little… subdued."

Maybe a little soul-baring was called for after all.

"Sometimes I have to work really hard not to let all this get to me," Shaun admitted. "Most of the time, I win." He mimicked Nathan's shrug. "Tonight, I'm losing."

Nathan placed his hand on Shaun's back. "Hey. It's okay. No one expects you to be Superman, all right? You've got a lot to cope with. Just don't cope with it all by yourself. That's what *I'm* here for." He rubbed up and down Shaun's spine with a gentle motion. "If it ever gets too much, and I'm not around, call me? I'm a good listener, and sometimes just letting it all spill out is all it takes to ease the burden. Because it *is* a burden, I know."

"You must have seen a lot of people like me."

Nathan nodded. "That's why I'm offering. When you're around Peter, does it feel as if you have to hide what you're going through, hide the hurt that slams into you when you see what he's becoming?" When Shaun nodded, his throat tight, Nathan gave another nod. "Well, you don't have to hide that from me, okay?" He smiled. "I've got broad shoulders. Lean on 'em if you need to."

"Thank you." Except those simple words weren't enough to convey Shaun's gratitude.

Nathan glanced at the countertop. "I gotta say, my version of mac and cheese is cook the macaroni, throw some cheese over it, then stick it in the oven."

Subject changed. That was fine by Shaun.

"I think I can improve on that." He filled a pot with water, and set it to boil, then turned on the oven. Then he grabbed the wooden chopping board from its hook on the wall and pulled a knife from the block. "So what do you usually do on a Saturday night?" He wanted to get the conversation back on an even keel.

Nathan snorted. "Veg out on the couch with popcorn, and watch a movie. Oh, and try to stop Cat from stealing pieces. He likes it." He paused as Shaun peeled away the onion's outer layer. "You put onion in it?"

"Mom used to say sautéed onion gave it a nice flavor. She let it kinda caramelize. And it's only half an onion." Shaun turned his head to look at him. "Is that a problem? Because if it is, I can leave it out."

Nathan smiled. "No problem at all. In fact, I can't wait to taste it."

Shaun cut into the onion half horizontally, then vertically before dicing it. "Something I've been meaning to ask you for a while. What's it like being a male nurse?"

Nathan laughed. "Wow. Do you want the long or the short answer?"

Shaun tipped the elbow macaroni into the bubbling water, then turned down the heat. He set the timer. "I was just curious, that's all. I mean, most nurses are female, right?"

Nathan let out an exaggerated sigh. "Okay. Here we go. The History of Male Nurses, as told to me by my course lecturer." When Shaun peered at him, he grinned. "Hey, if I had to sit through it, so can you."

Shaun inclined his head toward the fridge. "Help yourself to iced tea. Sounds as if you might need it." He unwrapped the slices of American cheese and cut them into narrow strips, then he grated the sharp Cheddar.

Nathan laughed. "Well, you asked." He got up and went over to the fridge. "She told us the first nursing school in the world was for men only, and it was in India in 250 BC. Then she went on about how men took care of the wounded during the 11th century Crusades. *And* staffed the field hospitals in the Franco-Prussian War of 1870."

"I'm assuming by this point you were all snoring," Shaun said with a smile. He dropped the butter into the frying pan. "I'm sure Florence Nightingale featured in this lecture somewhere."

"Oh yeah, she did—but only to mention that

Florence saw nursing as a female-only career." Nathan leaned against the fridge. "There were male nurses serving on the front line in World War I, with the same training and same diplomas as the female nurses, but the men only got half the pay. And after the war, you often saw male nurses working in mental health hospitals. They received little training, and the general view was they were less qualified and had a lower status than female nurses."

"Seriously?" Shaun shook his head. "It's funny if you think about it. Women talk about the glass ceiling, and not getting paid as much as men, but stuff like this doesn't get a mention."

"Uh-huh." Nathan retook his seat, and Shaun tipped the diced onion into the melted butter, pushing the pieces around the pan before leaving them to sauté. He measured out the flour. "Male nurses account for less than ten percent of all nurses in the US today," Nathan continued. "Mostly 'cause of the perception they'll have more difficulties in the workplace."

"And did *you*? When you worked in hospitals?"

"Yeah, a bit. People tend to see us in one of several roles. First off, there's the assumption that all male nurses are gay."

Shaun blinked. "Really?" When Nathan nodded, he grinned. "Er... you *are* gay."

Nathan laughed. "Yeah, but you only know that 'cause I *told* you. To be honest, I got it a lot from older male patients. It was worse years ago. Then the Vietnam medics came home and began attending nursing school. Only thing was, a lot of those medics didn't go into nursing, but became physicians' assistants. And so the myth persisted: *real* men became PAs—*gay* men became nurses." He smiled. "Having said that? Those older male patients sure appreciated having me around to help them stand to pee when they were post-surgery."

"I can understand that." Shaun stirred the flour into the onion, moving it with a whisk to prevent lumps from forming. He added milk, mustard, salt, and pepper. He let it cook until the mixture boiled and thickened, then added the cheeses, stirring until it all melted.

"And of course, I was the walking, talking lifting machine. You have *no* idea how many times a day I got asked to do some heavy physical activity."

Shaun bit back a smile. "Have you looked in a mirror lately? The size of you? Christ, your hands *dwarf* mine."

"Okay, you may have a point. But I also become a sort of security guard."

Shaun frowned. "What do you mean?"

"Patients nowadays are anything *but* patient. They can get violent, especially toward nurses. It's a shit deal, but it's happening more and more. They liked having me around, because while people were happy being aggressive toward a *female* nurse, once *I* came into the room, they backed off. I got good at de-escalating."

"That also might be because you nailed it the other day." When Nathan gave him a quizzical glance, Shaun smiled. "You're a calm person."

He chuckled. "I need to be. The number of times I was a new nurse on night duty, and some female nurse screamed because she thought I was an intruder. Or the times I had a patient say to me, 'Oh no, dear, I'd like a real nurse, please.'"

"But… you *are* a real nurse."

"*You* know that, and *I* know that, but… I kinda

expected that attitude from patients, but coworkers and the public could be just as bad. As a for instance... I started working in a new unit, on nights. The second day I was there, one of the day nurses kept bringing up the fact that I was a guy. I got tired of it. So... I put up with it for about a week, then I waited till she was in earshot before starting a conversation with a couple of other nurses. I told them I loved working in the unit, but I wished people would quit pointing out the obvious. Me being a guy was not relevant, and I just wanted to be treated like any other RN."

"What happened?"

Nathan smiled. "Didn't get another peep out of her. But dear *Lord*, the things some people said. I went out for a drink one night with five or six female nurses—I think it was someone's birthday. Anyhow, this guy came up to us, and started chatting to me. He said 'You work with these ladies or are you dating one of them?' I explained we were all nurses. So the guy stared at me—granted, he wasn't exactly sober—and then he asked 'Why didn't you become a doctor?' Y'know, it really is insulting. If a woman's a nurse, they're all 'Yay! Good for you, girl! You became a nurse." And what does a guy get? 'Good try, buddy—but you didn't become a doctor, did ya?' What does that imply? For a woman, it's some monumental achievement, but for a guy, it's somehow *lowering* yourself as a man?" Nathan grimaced. "One guy had the nerve to tell me I'd only become a nurse to see women naked."

Shaun stared. "What did you say to that?"

He smirked. "I told him women didn't do it for me, but *he* sure did. Then I puckered up. Never seen a guy move so fast." He drank some of his iced tea. "It wasn't *all* bad though. A bonus of being male was that I tended to be left out of the loop when it came to gossip. And sometimes it felt like I'd just gained seventy sisters." He leaned back in his chair. "That night we were out drinking? One of my coworkers took me aside once the drunken asshole had left us alone. She said no one outside of a hospital really knew half of what nurses did—but *we* did, and that was all that mattered."

Shaun turned off the heat and then drained the macaroni. He emptied the colander's contents into a baking dish before pouring the sauce over it. Nathan sniffed. "That smells amazing."

Shaun combined the pasta and sauce. "Mom's trick was to sprinkle it with Panko breadcrumbs." He reached into the cabinet for the packet, and shook it generously over the dish. "And now we shove it in the oven for a half hour." He smiled. "The hardest part is trying to get my dad to wait ten minutes once it's done. He wants to eat it right away."

"Who you talking to in there?" Dad hollered.

Shaun's gaze met Nathan's. "His timing…" He gestured to the countertop. "I'll clean up in here. You go say hi to him."

Nathan finished his tea and got up. "Sure there's nothing I can do to help?"

"Positive. Besides, he told me this evening he thinks you're a good boy."

"He tells me that too." Nathan walked toward the doorway. "And for the record, I think your dad's a special, sweet man." Then he went through the arch into the living room.

Shaun stared after him. *I think* you're *pretty special too.* He still couldn't get over Nathan being gay. And yet in their conversations, even after he'd shared about his friends' sexuality, Shaun had been careful to make no mention of his own. He knew why, of course.

Admitting he was gay felt like too close a step to admitting he was attracted to Nathan, and that just wasn't right, not when Nathan was there in a professional capacity.

He's never gonna know.

Chapter Seven

November 16

Nathan toweled Peter's head. "I bet that feels better." It had been the first time he'd shampooed Peter's hair while he was in his chair, but it had gone well. Peter was spending more time of late in his recliner, but he still wanted to go to the bathroom, instead of using the commode that sat in the corner, ready for action.

Nathan got that. The commode had to feel as if Peter had crossed a line, and maybe he wasn't ready for that. Except right then, Nathan had other matters on his mind.

Something was up.

Peter had refused to take his meds that morning, and every suggestion Nathan had made for an activity had been met with sounds of frustration and annoyance. He knew challenging behavior usually meant an unmet need—now all he had to do was figure out what Peter needed.

"Hey." Nathan kept his voice soft as he laid his hand gently on Peter's arm. "Want me to put on some music?" Peter loved piano music, and Nathan had gone through his CD collection, searching for anything that might help.

Peter looked him in the eye, and Nathan swallowed hard to see his confusion. "Where's Laura?"

Aw crap. It wasn't the first time he'd asked after

her, but the previous times Nathan had managed to deflect the question. Before he could respond, the front door opened, and Shaun came into the living room, rubbing his arms.

"It's snowed! Only a couple of inches." He bent to remove his boots, then set them on the mat beside the door.

Nathan chuckled. "Give it a month. You won't be sounding so happy when we've got ten inches or more."

Peter stared at Shaun, his eyes wide. "Where's your mom? She's been gone all day."

Shaun froze, and Nathan's heart went out to him. "You'd best tell him," he told Shaun quietly. "It'll be better coming from you."

Shaun walked over to Peter's chair and crouched in front of him. He covered Peter's hand with his, then took a deep breath. "Dad... Mom died. Nine years ago. I know you can't—"

"She isn't dead. I... I saw her last night."

Shaun's eyes glistened. "Dad... please... Mom died. She had cancer, remember?"

Peter gazed at him in such confusion that Nathan was close to tears himself. "She... she's gone?"

Shaun nodded, wiping his eyes. "It's just you and me now."

Peter let out a wail, pulled his hand free of Shaun's and reached for the wedding photo on the table. Nathan grabbed it and handed it to him, and Peter clutched it to his chest. "She can't be dead."

Shaun stood and laid his hand on Peter's shoulder, but Peter didn't register it. He held the frame to him, the tears coursing down his cheeks. "Dad," Shaun began, but Peter turned his head away.

"Leave me alone."

Nathan tugged Shaun's arm. "Come into the kitchen," he murmured. "Give him a little space. He'll be okay once he's calmed down. Right now you can't reach him."

Shaun followed him into the kitchen, and Nathan went straight to the kettle. Shaun sank onto one of the chairs and put his head in his hands. "It's as if she died all over again."

His voice... Shaun sounded beaten.

Don't you get down there in that hole with him. Lift him the fuck out of there.

Nathan filled the kettle and switched it on. "For Peter, that's *exactly* how it is. He's grieving as if he just lost her." He kept his tone even.

"What did he mean, he saw her last night?"

Nathan sighed. "That could be one of two things—his memory playing tricks on him, or..."

"Or what?"

He hesitated for a moment before responding. "A hallucination. You can get those with Alzheimer patients."

Shaun stared at him. "Wow. This disease really *is* the gift that keeps on giving, isn't it?" The note of bitterness in his voice was hard to hear.

"I'm assuming he's asked after your mom before now."

Shaun nodded. "I was a coward. I pretended I never heard the question."

"Hey." Nathan placed his hands flat to the table and gave Shaun a hard stare. "Now you listen to me. Wanting to avoid putting yourself through mental anguish does *not* make you a coward. It's more like... guarding your mental health. And don't think this won't happen again, because it will. That's the way it gets." He softened his voice. "And for the record? He's asked me before too, and I've always managed to deflect it, just like you did, but not this time."

"He seems to have gone downhill so fast. Is he… is he…?"

Nathan sensed where Shaun was going. "He's not at the end stage, not yet," he said as he straightened.

"How do you know?"

"Because…" Nathan counted off on his fingers. "He can still sit upright. That might not sound like much, but it is, trust me. He has *some* control of his bowels and bladder. He can still speak. Granted, the conversations are decreasing, but…" He pulled out a chair and sat facing Shaun. "There are no absolutes with this, okay? I've seen patients who were mid-stage suddenly shift to late stage just like that." He snapped his fingers. "But there *is* one thing you need to consider. It might be time to start pureeing his food." When Shaun blinked, Nathan continued. "He's finding it a little harder to swallow lately, so make it easy for him. You've got a stick blender, right? I saw it in a drawer. So use it. Anything to keep up his nourishment." The kettle beeped, and he stood. "I'm making you some tea, okay? And you're gonna drink it."

Shaun gave a half smile. "Yes, sir."

Nathan went to the cabinet and removed the box of tea bags. "And now I'm going to change the subject. Next week is Thanksgiving. You got any plans?"

"Beyond feeding my dad pureed turkey and cranberry sauce?" Shaun stared at the tabletop. "Thanksgiving is the last thing on my mind right now."

When the idea came to him, Nathan's heartbeat quickened. *She's gonna kill me.* But he knew it was the right thing to do. "I have a suggestion for you. See what you think. How would it be if I came here next week and cooked a meal for the three of us?" When silence fell, he turned to face Shaun.

"Why would you do that?" Shaun gaped.

"I'm not saying I'd cook a turkey with all the trimmings, just a simple meal that you don't have to think about. You won't be working, right? So you could spend the day with your dad, and I'd take care of both of you."

"I think you already do enough of that," Shaun murmured. "And I don't mean looking after my dad. You think I didn't notice?"

Nathan pasted on as innocent an expression as he could muster. "Notice what?"

Shaun gave him a glance that was an exact match for his momma's *Oh really?* look. "So who folded the laundry last week? Who vacuumed? Was it fairies?"

Shit.

"You're not paid to do those things."

"When I see a thing needs doing, I just do it," Nathan explained. The truth was too uncomfortable to share.

I want to take care of you. Shaun's friends would be having their own family get-togethers. *And this could be the last Thanksgiving with your dad.* Nathan wanted to make it as easy on Shaun as he could.

"Much as I'm grateful you'd even come up with such an idea, I'm sure there's somewhere else you should be. Won't your family miss you?"

"My momma will have a houseful. She'll be too busy cooking up a storm to miss me," Nathan lied.

He'd square it with her somehow. There was always Christmas…

"Shaun?" Peter called from the next room.

He was up and out of his chair in a heartbeat, dashing toward the living room. Nathan followed but hung back, waiting under the arch as Peter held his arms wide, and they hugged. Then he retreated into the kitchen to make them both something to eat, and to give them some space.

Maybe Momma can send me some of her recipes for soup. Nathan wanted to give Shaun the gift of time with his dad, and if that meant Shaun coming home and finding a pan of soup on the stove, then Nathan would make it happen.

As soon as Nathan walked through his front door, Cat was there, moving sinuously in and out between his ankles. "Oh, I guess you're hungry."

Cat turned his head up and let out a long plaintive meow.

Nathan chuckled. "That was you saying 'Ya think?'" He stepped into the small kitchen and headed for the fridge where Cat's opened tin of cat food sat covered with a red plastic lid. Nathan forked it into the empty bowl, then grabbed the dry food and shook that over it. He straightened to fill the water bowl and Cat was there, faster than a heat-seeking missile. "Dear *Lord*, Cat, you can move when you want to."

Nathan left him to it and went back into the living room. He sank onto the couch and got his phone out. There was little use in delaying the inevitable. He hit speed dial, and Momma's face filled the screen. *Here goes…*

"Hey. You just got home from work?"

"Yeah. Listen, Momma, you think you could send me some of your soup recipes? You know, the ones you used to make for Granddaddy? There was a chicken and dumpling one, bacon-potato corn chowder, that ham and beans one he loved—and the one you used to call the South in a pot."

"You takin' up cooking? Since when?"

"Remember I told you about my patient, the one with Alzheimer's? They're for him. It's getting tricky for him to swallow, and I thought of your soups." They'd still need pureeing, but it was something he could prepare while Shaun was at work, and when Peter was napping.

"Aw. Sure. I'll look 'em up."

"Thanks. And while I've got you…" He took a deep breath. "Momma, I won't be spending Thanksgiving with you. I just can't. I… I've got too much going on here. I'll be there for Christmas, I promise. Besides, you'll need me to put the angel on top of the Christmas tree, won't you?"

"You kids are never gonna let me forget that, are you? It was only one time."

"Yeah, the one time you stood on a chair to put it up there, lost your balance, and sent the whole tree flying. Thank God you always put the angel on first, or you'd have smashed every ornament."

"Don't change the subject. And the only reason you put the angel on top of the tree is because you take after your Daddy, and Jadyn and Phoebe take after me."

"You mean, you three are short. Tell it like it is, Momma."

She sighed, and he steeled himself for either a backlash or a guilt trip. "I know you'd be here if you could, so… it's okay. I can wait till Christmas."

"Wait… what?" He'd expected more of a battle.

"You're a grown man. I'm not gonna yell at you or insist you be here."

It's never stopped you before. "Thanks, Momma. You'll have plenty to do with everyone else who'll be there. And I'm sure Phoebe would love to help out in the kitchen."

"Are you serious? Child, you *know* your sister can burn water."

He chuckled. "Remember the pigs in blankets that one year?"

"Oh, dear God, don't." She paused. "You sure you can get time off for the holidays?"

"I already booked myself three days." He'd found a nurse who was willing to cover for him, if Shaun needed it. Except there was a little voice in his head that whispered maybe a nurse wouldn't be required. Maybe there would be no patient to care for.

A lot could happen between Thanksgiving and Christmas.

It was a sad thought, but a realistic one. If Peter deteriorated, a hospice would be the best place for him, and all the signs were there that such an event could be imminent.

He'll be here for Thanksgiving. And Nathan would be there for Shaun.

"Okay, go eat. You must be tired. I'll rustle up those recipes and email them to you." Another pause.

"You're going to a lot of trouble for this patient."

"He's worth it." So was Shaun.

"I hope his son appreciates all the effort you're going to."

Nathan didn't want Shaun thinking like that—he wanted Shaun to concentrate on his dad.

While he still can.

Chapter Eight

November 25

Nathan woke with a start as sharp claws engaged with his bare chest. "Cat, what the fuck?" He lifted Cat off and dropped him to the rug. "You can't be that hungry at this hour." He glanced at his alarm clock, then glared at the tabby. "It's seven o'clock, you furbag. And I don't recollect asking for a furry alarm call on my day off either."

Then he heard it. Someone was ringing his doorbell. Insistently.

Now what?

"Someone's gonna lose a finger," he muttered as he got out of bed and pulled on his robe. "Coming!" He hurried through the apartment to his front door, yanked back the bolt, and— "Oh my God."

Momma was standing on his doormat.

Nathan gaped. "Momma, what are you doing here?"

"'Bout time you got up. I'm freezing out here." She crossed the threshold, giving him the sweet smile that always said she was up to something. "Mornin', Mohammed. How you doin'? I'm that mountain you keep avoiding."

"Momma, I said I'd visit you at Christmas. You agreed."

"I changed my mind. Now close the damn door. You're letting all the heat out and the snow in."

She kicked off her shoes, then barged past him, glancing at her surroundings before peering through the door into the kitchen. "Good Lord, how am I supposed to cook a Thanksgiving dinner in a kitchen no bigger than your daddy's shed?"

"Thanksgi—Momma, what are you talking about?" He shivered, and closed the door. "It's only seven o'clock."

"Mm-hm. I saw the sunrise about fifteen minutes ago. Very pretty. And I got up way before dawn to pack the car with everything I'd need to cook my eldest son's Thanksgiving dinner." She chuckled. "You'll have leftovers for a month."

"But... Jadyn... Phoebe..." *This has to be a dream.* Except it was starting to feel more like a nightmare.

Momma put her hands on her hips. "I drive for over an hour to get here—through snow, I might add—and you don't even have a kiss for your momma?"

He walked over to her, bent down, and kissed her cheek. "Morning, Momma. Now *please*, tell me what's going on."

She sighed. "I spoke with Jadyn and Phoebe last week, right after you called. I told them I was coming here, and they were all for it. They send you their love, by the way." She clicked her tongue. "Your kitchen is tiny, but I'll manage. It'll be fun, just the two of us."

Oh God.

Nathan went into the kitchen to set up the coffee pot. He was going to need it. "Momma, it's a great idea, but... I won't be here tomorrow." He couldn't hold back. "Which I could've told you if you'd called to let me know what you were planning."

Momma stood in the doorway, her eyes glacial. "You're going someplace? After everything you said about not being able to visit your own family?"

"No, Momma... it's not like that." He poured water into the reservoir, then picked up the box of filters. "I'm going to cook a meal for Peter and his son Shaun. Nothing fancy, but that way they get to spend time together."

She fell silent for a moment. Nathan got on with spooning coffee into the filter, his heart pounding. *This is a mess.*

"Peter... he's your patient?"

Nathan nodded. "But seeing as you're here, and you've gone to so much trouble, I'll call Shaun and cancel. He'll be——"

"No, don't do that," she interjected. "I've got a better idea. I'll cook dinner for all of us."

Okay, this was getting weirder. "What?"

She widened her eyes. "Well, I've got all this food. You think I'm gonna feed it to your cat? Think about it. I'd be in the kitchen, cooking, and you and this... Shaun could spend the day with Peter."

"You can't do that."

She blinked. "Oh really? You wanna try stopping me?" The twinkle in her eyes faded. "Peter... is he close?"

Nathan nodded.

"Then that does it. Make it a good day for him." Her eyes clouded over. "I remember the last Thanksgiving with your granddaddy. I don't think he knew what day it was." She straightened. "Only... you'd best check with Shaun that this is okay."

"I'll call him after I'd had some coffee." Nathan bit his lip. "Then I'd better give some thought to where you're sleeping tonight."

She laughed. "That's easy. I'm the momma. I get the bed, *you* get the couch." She patted his cheek. "Now put some clothes on and help me bring in all the bags."

"Just how many bags are there?" Nathan asked as he headed for his bedroom.

"Put it this way. We won't do it in one trip," she called out.

Dear Lord, they wouldn't fit in the kitchen.

Nathan grabbed his phone from the nightstand and composed a short text.

Need to talk. Let me know when it's convenient.

He dropped the phone onto the bed, squirmed into his jeans and pulled on a sweater. As he put on his socks, there was a *ping*.

Awake. Had coffee. Will that do?

Nathan smiled to himself. He clicked Call. "Good morning. You need to be sitting down for this."

"Oh God. What?"

"You know I was going to come over tomorrow and cook dinner?"

"You can't make it?" Nathan couldn't miss the note of disappointment in Shaun's voice.

"Not exactly… I'm still coming, but… I won't be alone, and I won't be the one cooking."

"Okay, you have my full attention. What's going on?"

Nathan explained the situation, and there was silence from Shaun's end. "Shaun? You still there?"

He caught Shaun's soft sigh. "Your mom sounds as if she's a wonderful person. But is she sure about this? I mean, cooking for two strangers…"

Nathan chuckled. "Trust me. By the end of

tomorrow? You won't be strangers anymore. And never mind if Momma is sure about this—are you?"

"I love it. Dad might be a little confused though. Thank your mom for me. I guess I'll see you both tomorrow. I'm gonna go find Mom's best tablecloth and candlesticks."

"You do that. I'm gonna change the bedding for Momma. Me and Cat will be on the couch tonight."

Shaun laughed. "Make Cat sleep in his basket."

Nathan snorted. "I can tell you've never met Cat." He disconnected.

"Coffee's ready," Momma hollered.

Thank God for that. Nathan reckoned he'd need it fed to him intravenously by the end of the day, because Momma was not one to sit and watch TV. She'd be doing something, and Nathan laid even money it would impact on him.

Momma came out of the kitchen. "What's Shaun's kitchen like?"

"Bigger than mine." Nathan sat on the couch, Cat curled up in his lap, asleep. Nathan hadn't bothered switching on the TV: Momma would only turn it off again.

She cackled. "That's not saying much." She sat in Nathan's armchair.

"It reminds me of grandma's. Lots of countertops, a double oven…The table's in there too."

Momma gave her forehead an exaggerated swipe. "Thank goodness. There isn't enough room to swing a cat in yours." She glanced at Cat. "And you can relax, furball. That wasn't a suggestion." She peered at the living room. "Well, this looks better than it did when I arrived this morning."

"Hey, it didn't need cleaning, okay?" he protested. She'd spent the day tidying, rearranging... Hell, he'd gone into his closet to find she'd refolded all his clothes in their drawers, and arranged his hangers so the longest items were at one end.

She held up her hands. "You're right. I obviously trained you well."

Nathan laughed. "Talk about a backhanded compliment."

"I'd say this apartment needs a woman's touch, but that ship hasn't just sailed, it never made it into the harbor." Momma cocked her head to one side. "How long have you lived here? Ten years? Twelve?"

"Something like that."

She nodded. "And in all that time... have you been alone?"

Nathan gestured to Cat. "Nope. He's been here for seven of those years."

Momma narrowed her gaze. "You know what I mean. I'm assuming you've been... out since you moved to Portland? That *is* the right word, isn't it?"

"Yes, Momma, it is, yeah, I'm out, and yeah, it's been just me here." He hadn't made a decision to be single—it was the way things had worked out.

"Are there any... places you can go to?"

He smiled. "Momma, you talking about gay bars?" She nodded. "There are a few. Ogunquit's got a couple, Portland too, or so I've heard. I haven't visited any of them."

"Why not? How are you supposed to meet people if you don't go where they're at?"

"Gay bars aren't really my thing."

She arched her eyebrows. "And what *is* your 'thing'?"

"Staying in. Sitting by the fire. Watching a movie." He raised his glass. "Some wine." Cat meowed, and Nathan stroked his back. "A cat in my lap." He took a mouthful of white wine.

Momma sighed. "Sweetheart, if you're gonna get anywhere, there needs to be a guy's head in your lap, not a damn cat."

Holy fuck.

Cat was off him in a flash as wine spattered his fur. "Christ, Momma... Warn a guy before you say stuff like that." Nathan wiped his lips.

"Don't you go taking the Lord's name in vain. And I didn't mean... Lord, where is your mind? In the gutter? When your daddy and I were first married, he used to sit at one end of the couch, and I'd stretch out with my head in his lap. He'd stroke my hair... We'd spend hours like that."

Nathan smiled. "I like the sound of that."

"So why don't you have someone special in your life? You too picky? Is that it?" She shook her head. "Your brother was the same. Remember how he'd bring his girlfriends to Sunday lunch? They were all nice girls, but not one of them lasted more than a week. By the time Della showed up, I was losing hope."

Nathan recalled Jadyn confiding in him that Della was the only girl Momma had taken an instant liking to, and he wondered if that had had something to do with him finally settling down.

"I'm not picky. It's just that… so far, pickings have been a little slim. I don't get to meet many guys—"

"And you never will if you stay home all the time," Momma retorted.

Cat stepped back into his lap, turned three times in a circle, then settled down, his tail over his paws. Nathan scritched him under his chin, and Cat's purr rumbled through him.

"You're forty-three, son. You work hard, caring for all these people… But you need someone to care for you. To be there for you. It can't be an easy job. I imagine it's heartbreaking sometimes."

"Yeah, it is." Nathan would get to know someone, form a bond with them, only to lose them when death stepped in and led them away. It was an emotional release for those closest to the deceased, and mixed feelings for him.

Walking away when Peter's time came was going to be doubly hard.

"You need someone who understands your job. You support your patient and their family—you need someone who'll support you." A heavy sigh rolled from her lips. "I just want you to be happy, baby."

"I know, Momma."

"And you'd tell me, wouldn't you, if you were interested in someone?"

He gave her a frank stare. "We talked about this. I'm not dating anyone."

"I didn't say dating, I said if you were interested in a guy."

Nathan went with the truth. "Momma… I don't want to be alone, okay? I'm tired of coming home to an empty apartment. I'm tired of cooking for one. I'm tired of not having anyone to argue with over the remote. Or complain about when they hog the covers. And yes, I'd like kids too, before I get too old to play with them, but most guys these days aren't into that. The few men I've dated? They live to party. They don't want... complications." He smiled. "But I promise you, if I ever meet a guy who's a homebody, loves kids and cats, and wants some of his own? I'll bring him to meet you."

"You'd better." Momma glanced at the clock and yawned. "I'm gonna go to bed. Got a long day ahead of us tomorrow." She peered at the neat pile of sheets and blankets at the other end of the couch, topped with a pillow. "You gonna be warm enough in here?"

He grinned. "I'll have my own furry hot water bottle."

She stood. "Then I'll say goodnight." Momma walked over to him, bent low, and kissed his cheek. "Sweet dreams, baby." She straightened and headed for the bedroom.

Nathan stroked Cat's head. "Now don't go digging your claws into me during the night, you hear?" His thoughts went to Shaun. *I hope he and Peter had a good day.*

Nathan would do his best to ensure the following day was the best he could make it—for both Peter *and* Shaun.

Chapter Nine

November 26

Shaun stared at all the bags Nathan and his mom had brought into the kitchen via the back door. "Mrs. Simpson, just how much food do you plan on cooking?"

Mrs. Simpson laughed. "It took one bag for the turkey. I hope you like turkey because you're going to be living on it for weeks."

"I think Nathan will be taking some of it home with him," Shaun remarked. "But seriously… what are we having?" It seemed like an awful lot of food for one meal.

"Roast turkey, stuffing, mashed potatoes, green beans, corn, cranberry sauce, biscuits—"

Nathan froze in the act of placing a bag onto the countertop. "Momma… tell me you're making your buttermilk biscuits."

She smiled. "Now, would it be Thanksgiving without them?" Then she turned to Shaun. "And we'll have no more of this Mrs. Simpson business. I'm Cassie, okay?"

He wasn't about to argue with her. Nathan had stated his mom ruled, and having met her, Shaun could see why. Cassie was quite a character. "Yes… Cassie."

She beamed. "Great. I'll make sure no one goes hungry today, but I do ask that y'all stay out of the kitchen. I don't want you boys under my feet while I'm cooking."

"You've got it."

"Why don't you show Momma where everything is, and I'll go see Peter?" Nathan suggested.

"That would be best. He's been more confused than usual this morning. He asked me again where Mom was."

Nathan squeezed his shoulder. "Then I'll keep him company while you give Momma the guided tour." He left the room.

Cassie surveyed the kitchen. "Okay... let's see what we've got here." Shaun opened drawers to reveal their contents, then the cabinets with all the pots and pans. She peeked into the fridge and nodded in approval. "Plenty of room in there. Good. Where do you keep your roasting pans?"

Shaun pointed to another cabinet. "In there."

She smiled. "I think I've seen everything I need to." She hoisted a bag onto the countertop and began removing the items.

"This is really kind of you." Except kind came nowhere near to expressing how he felt.

Cassie turned around. "It's okay. I know your head is probably in a spin right now, isn't it? What you're going through is tough. So if I can lighten the load a little..." Her voice was warm.

Shaun recollected what Nathan had said. "Oh. Was it *your* dad who had Alzheimer's?"

She nodded. "Nathan may know about treating patients with dementia, but I probably understand better than he does how it feels to have a parent going through this. Any time you need a hug, sweetheart? You holler."

Tears pricked Shaun's eyes. "How about right

now?"

Cassie held her arms wide, and Shaun didn't hesitate. She held him close, her cheek warm against his. She was shorter than he was, but her arms enveloped him and hugged him tightly. When she released him, both of them wiped their eyes. "Now I'll put on some coffee. I brought cookies from home too." Her eyes sparkled. "Wanna see the definition of a New York minute? Watch Nathan when he sees the cookies."

Shaun laughed. "I'm guessing he likes them?"

"*Like*? Honey, he'd bite off your fingers for one of my chocolate chip cookies." She paused. "How about your dad? Will he cope with the dinner?"

Shaun sighed. "I've been pureeing his food for a week now, ever since he complained food was sticking in his throat, and that it hurt to swallow. He even coughs a little when he drinks."

"Don't you worry none. I'll puree his dinner." She tilted her head to one side. "Can he still feed himself?"

"Yeah, but... slowly. A couple of times I offered to feed him, but that didn't go down so well. Rather like his food."

"Don't worry if he takes his time. This meal will take a while to eat, believe me."

Shaun stared at all the ingredients that covered the countertops. "Are you making everything from scratch?"

"Not everything. I bought the pumpkin pie at the store." She gave him another warm smile. "Let me get myself sorted, and then I'll shout when the coffee's ready." She patted his arm. "Go spend time with your dad. I've got this."

Shaun was halfway to the door when he stopped. "When Nathan called to say you were coming, I had no idea you'd be doing so much." He swallowed. "It's been a long time since there was a proper Thanksgiving dinner in this house. So… thank you." Then he headed through the arch to find a movie to make his dad smile.

Shaun had already found his smile—Nathan and his mom had brought it with them.

Shaun and Peter were watching a DVD, and Shaun had clearly chosen well: every now and then Peter laughed, and the joy on Shaun's face lightened Nathan's heart. The only sound coming from the kitchen had been his momma's singing. He crept through the arch and came to a halt in the doorway, watching her as she peered into a pan from which steam rose. Her happy little hum brought back memories of childhood.

"How's it going?" he asked, strolling into the room.

"We're almost there. The potatoes are mashed, the beans and corn are done, the gravy is simmering, the stuffing is being kept warm in the oven, along with the biscuits, and the turkey is resting under there." She pointed to a mound of tin foil.

Nathan went to it and peeked underneath, yowling when she smacked his butt. "Hey!"

"Hey nothing. I remember when you were a kid. Every time you went into the kitchen at Thanksgiving, I made you whistle."

"Yeah. Why was that?"

She snickered. "Seriously? Because if you were whistling, you weren't eating. *You* may not remember blaming the dog for the fact that there was less cooked turkey than there should have been, but *I* do." She nodded toward the doorway. "Close the door a sec, would you?"

Nathan did as instructed. "Is anything wrong?"

Momma leaned against the countertop, a dish towel in her hands. "You know when you finally admitted you were gay, and I told you I already knew? And don't you be calling me Sister Rose again, you hear?"

"Yes, Momma."

"And I said I had a premonition about you having your eye on some white boy?"

"Yes," he said, drawing out the syllable. *No. She can't mean...*

She inclined her head in the direction of the living room. "He's right in there, isn't he?"

God damn his momma and her instincts.

"I don't know what you're talking about." Even as he uttered the words, he knew it was useless. He couldn't hide a bean from her, and they both knew it.

Momma folded her arms. "Really? You're gonna stand there and lie to your mother? I'm not blind."

Nathan didn't trust himself to speak.

"Is Shaun gay?"

There was no escape. "I don't know, and I'm not gonna ask."

"Well, how are you gonna find out if you don't?"

Nathan huffed. "Look, it doesn't matter if he's gay, straight, bi, whatever. Nothing's gonna happen between us."

"Why not?"

He rolled his eyes. "Can you say professionalism? Immoral conduct? Ethics?"

Her eyes bulged. "So you're gonna keep your mouth shut?"

"Uh-huh. He doesn't need to know. He's got enough to cope with." He narrowed his gaze. "And why are you pushing this?"

Momma placed the dish towel on a hook by the sink. "I like him," she said simply. "He's been in and out of here all day, and I've seen enough to know he's polite, sweet, a little shy till he gets to know a person, and then he just... blossoms. He's kind, considerate. Okay, he wasn't what I envisaged for you, but we won't go there. If that's where your heart leads you..."

"My *heart* isn't leading me anywhere because this particular road leads *nowhere*."

"Fine. You just be in denial all you want. In the meantime, go get Peter ready for dinner. I want to set the table." She made a shooing motion with her hands. "Go on."

Shaking his head, Nathan stood and left the kitchen.

Mothers...

The kitchen table had been transformed. Mom's best snow-white tablecloth covered the blue surface, and the candlesticks that had been a wedding present stood between the serving dishes. The turkey looked bronze and succulent, and the air was filled with enticing aromas. Shaun sat facing his dad, and his awed expression tightened Shaun's throat.

Nathan lit the candles. "This is amazing, Momma."

Cassie beamed. "I hope it all tastes as good as it looks."

Nathan snorted. "Since when has your cooking ever been anything less than perfect?"

She coughed. "You never got to taste my first try at meringues, but let's not go there."

Nathan reached toward the plate of biscuits, and she picked up a large wooden spoon from beside her glass, and popped his hand with it.

"Ow. What was that for? And why did you bring that to the table?"

She widened her eyes. "Because I knew you'd go for the biscuits. I don't care whose house we're in— we don't touch a thing before we say grace."

Shaun wanted to laugh and cry at the same time. The playful banter was a reminder of family meals in the past, and it had been a while since he'd sat down to a proper Thanksgiving meal.

This is the last one, isn't it? The last one with his

dad, at any rate.

Cassie held out her hands, and Shaun took one. Dad didn't need to be told what to do: he grasped Cassie's and Nathan's, and Shaun closed the circle. Cassie bowed her head, and Shaun closed his eyes. Cassie's quiet voice broke the ensuing silence.

"Our Father in Heaven, we give thanks for the pleasure of gathering together for this occasion. We give thanks for this food prepared by loving hands. We give thanks for life, the freedom to enjoy it all, and all other blessings."

Shaun couldn't swallow.

"As we partake of this food, we pray for health and strength to carry on and try to live as You would have us. This we ask in the name of Christ, our heavenly Father. Amen."

Shaun whispered, "Amen," and Nathan's hand tightened on his. When Cassie released his hand, he quickly wiped away his tears, then gazed at the feast before them.

"*Now* can I have a biscuit?" Nathan's voice held a little whine that was so cute.

Cassie laughed. "No, you get to carve the turkey. And make a quick job of it, you hear? You're not a surgeon, you're a nurse, so just cut the damn bird."

Shaun's gaze met his dad's across the table, and warmth flooded through him as Dad mouthed *Happy Thanksgiving, son.*

"Happy Thanksgiving, Dad."

One look at his dad told Shaun he was flagging. He'd eaten, but not enough to make Shaun happy. In the end, he told himself to stop fighting the inevitable.

"Dad? You want to take a nap?"

Dad let out a sigh. "Could I?"

"Of course you can."

Dad gave Cassie a smile. "Thanks again. It was great."

"You're welcome, Peter. Go rest. We'll be here when you wake up."

"I've got this." Nathan put down his napkin and helped Dad to stand. With one strong arm around him, Nathan met Shaun's gaze. "You stay here with Momma. I'll get him settled, then I'll be right back." He guided Dad out of the kitchen, and it almost broke Shaun's heart to see Dad's shuffling gait.

"How long has it been since his diagnosis?" Cassie asked in a low voice.

"Nine years." He couldn't tear his eyes away from the doorway.

"It hurts, I know."

"Nathan's been a godsend," Shaun admitted. "A real rock."

"How old are you, Shaun?"

"Twenty-six. I'll be twenty-seven at New Year's." Shaun dragged his attention back to his dinner, but his appetite seemed to have dwindled.

"Nathan says you're a server in a restaurant in

Portland. Do you like your job?"

"Yeah. It's a family-run business, and they're good people. I got a job with them right out of high school."

"Didn't you want to go to college?"

Shaun took a mouthful of wine before replying. "I couldn't think about that, not when Mom was… And after, I didn't want to leave Dad on his own, so I got a job to keep me local."

"Do you think you'll stay a server?"

Shaun leaned back in his chair. "I haven't thought about it." He glanced up as Nathan returned to the table. "Is he okay?"

"Yeah, he's just worn out." Nathan retook his seat.

"I'm too busy living in the *now* to think about what might happen," Shaun told Cassie.

She pulled a biscuit apart and ate a small piece. "Ever thought about having kids?"

Something flashed across Nathan's face, and Cassie obviously saw it too. "Hey, I can ask," she retorted. "Some people know right off the bat that they don't want kids. Others can't wait. I was just curious to see which camp Shaun was in."

"I'd like kids. Maybe two or three."

"Greedy," Cassie commented with a smile.

"I grew up an only child, so did my mom and dad. I like the idea of a big family. I've seen photos of your grandkids. They're adorable."

Cassie beamed. "Aren't they cunning?"

Shaun laughed. "Careful. You're starting to sound like a Mainer." Everyone laughed at that.

"Of course, there's room in my heart for more." She shrugged. "I can wait."

Nathan coughed and muttered, "Pushing…"

Cassie merely smiled at him. "Now, please eat something. You haven't even scratched the surface."

Nathan caught his eye. "Peter wouldn't want to ruin your Thanksgiving," he murmured. He picked up a plate from the center of the table. "Besides, you haven't tried one of Momma's buttermilk biscuits."

"That's what *you* think." Shaun took one. "This'll be my second." He gazed at them. "I can't thank both of you enough for today. It was like being part of a family again."

Cassie's eyes glistened. "You're welcome, sweetheart. Now, you eat, but leave a little room for the pumpkin pie. Not that it will hold a candle to mine."

Nathan chuckled. "I don't doubt it."

"Can you both stay a while after we've finished eating?" Shaun wanted the day to last as long as possible.

Cassie cackled. "You think I'm gonna be able to move right away? I intend finding a comfy spot on the couch and not budging for at least an hour or two. You boys can deal with the dirty dishes."

When Nathan's jaw dropped, Shaun chuckled. "I think we'll let the dishwasher deal with 'em." When Cassie got up to go to the bathroom, he smiled. "I really like your mom."

"Trust me, the feeling is mutual." Nathan raised his wine glass. "Happy Thanksgiving, Shaun."

Shaun raised his own, and they clinked glasses. "Happy Thanksgiving, Nathan."

K.C. WELLS

Chapter Ten

November 30

Nathan let himself in by the back door as usual, to find Shaun sitting at the kitchen table, nursing a cup of coffee. He glanced up and gave a weary smile. "Good morning."

"Doesn't look much like one from where I'm standing," Nathan observed. "You okay?" He stomped his feet on the mat before removing his boots and coat.

Shaun waved a hand. "Just tired. Dad didn't have a good night. I think he had a nightmare. He was shouting about the house being on fire, and how he couldn't breathe. I sat with him till he fell asleep. That was a few hours ago." He drank from his cup. "He's still asleep. I didn't wanna wake him."

"Can you call in sick? You look like you could use some sleep yourself."

"Nice idea, but no. It's only six hours."

"Tell you what. When you get home, go to bed for a few hours. I'll stay with Peter. Even a little shuteye will help." Nathan couldn't do much, but he could do that.

"Thank you." Shaun gestured to the coffee pot. "Help yourself. I think I'm gonna need it fed intravenously today."

Nathan poured himself a cup, and joined Shaun at the table. "Before you ask, yes, Momma has gone home. She went last night." He'd felt awful leaving her in the apartment while he worked over the weekend, but she'd claimed it wasn't a problem. When he'd arrived home Saturday night, she had her feet up on the couch, Cat in her lap, and was plowing her way through his DVD collection. She even said the rest was exactly what she'd needed.

Nathan chuckled. "Leaving her alone in the apartment was a bad move."

"Why?"

"Man, she cleans *everything*. And then she cleans it again."

Shaun smiled. "She's just looking after her baby, that's all."

"Thank God she and Cat got along. Mind you, when she first arrived, Cat was looking at her like 'Who the hell is this in *my* apartment?'"

"When will you see her next?"

"Christmas. I'll go spend a few days with her and the rest of the family. If I don't, she'll have my balls made into baubles—probably with holly wrapped around them."

Shaun winced. Then his expression grew solemn. "I'm a little worried about Dad. I might need to call the doctor out."

"Anything specific I need to be aware of?"

"He was wheezing a little last night before he went to bed. And he seemed so tired."

"I'll see how he is when he wakes up. If he's still the same, I'll call the doc."

"Thank you." Shaun's face glowed. "I seem to be saying that a lot to you lately. I can't thank you and your mom enough for Thanksgiving."

"Who'd have thought Momma turning up unannounced could have such a wonderful result?"

Nathan glanced at the clock. "Hey, you need to be out of here."

"I haven't cleaned up my breakfast dishes yet," Shaun protested.

"Let me deal with those. You get to work. And don't push yourself too hard today, all right?"

Shaun's eyes twinkled. "Now I know where you get it from—your mom. You're very similar." He got up from the table. "I'll go brush my teeth, then I'll be out from under your feet."

Nathan arched his eyebrows. "You are *never* under my feet, you hear?"

"Thanks for that." Shaun left the room.

Nathan collected Shaun's cup and went to the sink to wash the dishes. His mind wasn't on the mundane chore, however, but on Peter. Wheezing, fatigue, more confusion… these were not good. He decided to call the doc anyway, whatever Peter's state when he awoke.

Five minutes later, Shaun was out of the house, and Nathan retrieved his medical kit before going to Peter's room. He opened the door, and the sound of Peter's wheezing breaths set his heart racing.

That does not sound good.

Nathan stood beside the bed. "Peter. Peter." When there was no response, he gave Peter's shoulder a gentle shake. "Hey, Peter. Time to wake up now." He laid his hand on Peter's forehead, and it was clammy—and warm.

Too warm.

"Hmm?" Peter half-opened his eyes.

Nathan removed his stethoscope and forehead thermometer from his kit. "Peter, I need to listen to your chest, okay?" When Peter gave a slight nod,

Nathan pulled back the comforter, then unfastened the buttons on Peter's pajama top. He placed the ends of the stethoscope in his ears, and placed the diaphragm just below the left clavicle before moving it to the right. He worked his way down Peter's chest, checking breath sounds in his upper and middle lobes. When he got to the lower lobes, he couldn't miss the coarse crackling sound, like Velcro being pulled apart.

Ah shit. Nathan knew what *that* meant.

He placed the forehead thermometer against Peter's brow, and when the reading flashed up, he groaned. He closed the flaps of the pajama top. "I'll be right back, okay?" Then he stepped outside the room and reached into his pocket for his phone.

"911, what's your emergency?"

He spoke quickly and clearly. "I need an ambulance. Male, fifty-nine years old, late-stage Alzheimer's. He has a fever of 103.6." He paused. "He's suffering from severe respiratory distress. It could be aspiration." That would account for the wheezing and the fever.

"What relation are you?"

"I'm his in-home nurse." He rattled off the address.

"Paramedics are on their way. They'll take him to the Maine Medical Center. Is there someone you should call?"

"His son. I'll do that once he's on his way." Thank God the Medical Center was close to where Shaun worked. When the call was over, Nathan disconnected and went back into Peter's room.

"Shaun," Peter croaked. "Laura."

"They're not here, Peter, but I am. Help is coming, okay?" And he wasn't going to budge from

Peter's side until he absolutely had to.

Shaun came back into the kitchen, stifling a yawn. Jean, Sandy's wife, let out a chuckle. "Someone needs a nap." She came in a couple of times a month to do the accounts. Apart from Shaun and another server, everyone who worked in the restaurant was part of one family.

"Maybe coffee instead?" he suggested. His phone vibrated in his pocket, and he pulled it out. When he saw it was Nathan, cold stole over him. "What's wrong?" Nathan did *not* call him at work.

"An ambulance just took your dad to Maine Med. I'm following in my car. Can you get there ASAP?"

"What's wrong with him?" His heart pounded.

"Tell you when you get here, okay? I'll be waiting by the main entrance."

"I'm coming now." He disconnected, his chest tingling, shivers coursing through him.

"Shaun, is it your dad?" Jean was at his side in a heart. "Is he at home?"

"On his way to Maine Med." He fumbled in his pocket for his car keys.

Jean took them from him. "You're in no state to drive. I'll do it. I can walk back after. Let's go."

Shaun's face grew warm. "Thank you."

Sandy held out his coat. "I hope he's okay. Let

us know what's happening, please? And if you need time off, it's not a problem."

Shaun slipped his arms into his coat sleeves, his throat suddenly constricted. He led Jean out of the restaurant and headed for his car. He couldn't speak. His stomach churned, his mouth dry. It wasn't far to the hospital, and once Jean had pulled into a parking space and switched off the engine, she went to hand him the keys, but he wouldn't take them.

"Drive back to the restaurant. I'll get a ride with Nathan. You've got too much to do without taking time out for me. Just leave the car in the Fore Street garage."

"Want me to come in with you?"

He shook his head. "Nathan will be there. Thanks again."

Jean leaned over and kissed his cheek. "Go to your dad."

He got out of the car, and Jean drove away. Shaun walked briskly toward the entrance. Once inside, he spotted Nathan instantly, and hurried over to him.

"What happened?"

"They're assessing him now. He has a fever of 103.6, and he's sweating profusely. That points to infection." Nathan took Shaun's arm and guided him along the hallway toward the Emergency Room. "Let's see what the docs say, all right?"

Shaun's head was spinning. "But where's the infection come from?"

"The most likely scenario is, he forgot to swallow when he was eating, and breathed in some food that went down his airway."

Shaun thought back to the previous evening. "But when could this have happened? Wouldn't I have noticed? Wouldn't he cough or something?" *What did I miss?*

"Symptoms of aspiration can occur right after eating, or they can happen over time, and you're correct—you would have noticed. Except some people who aspirate don't have any symptoms." Nathan's hand was at his back. "This isn't your fault, Shaun. If he'd shown any signs, you'd have seen it."

"You can't be sure of that."

They arrived at the waiting room, and Nathan ushered him to a seat. "Here. Sit. They're treating his respiratory distress right now. I've already given them Peter's details and I've made sure they know he has late-stage Alzheimer's," Nathan murmured. "They'll come find us."

Shaun sank into the chair, feeling dizzy. Nathan joined him. "I should've got him up this morning," Shaun muttered. "I should've realized—"

"Stop that. It isn't helping. Right now he's in the best place, okay?"

Shaun gazed around him at the faces of the people waiting for their own news. There was a TV monitor on the wall, but no one was watching.

We're all lost in our own worlds.

The door opened, and a doctor came into the room. "Mr. Clark?"

Shaun was on his feet in a heartbeat, hurrying over to him. "Doctor, how is he?" Nathan followed.

The doctor drew them aside to a quiet corner of the room, then gestured to the chairs. Shaun didn't want to sit—he wanted to see his dad. The gentle pressure of Nathan's hand on his shoulder, however, told him to do as the doctor wished.

The doctor referred to a tablet in his hand. "His

fever and breathing difficulties are the result of an infection. This has led to aspiration pneumonia. Aspiration is—"

"It's okay," Shaun interjected. "I know what that is. What are you going to do about it?" He took a breath. "I'm sorry, Doctor…" Shaun peered at his badge. "Doctor Sharma. That was rude."

"But understandable in the circumstances. His breathing needed assistance, so we've already started him on BiPAP."

"BiPAP? Isn't that like a ventilator?"

"Yes. It helps him breathe. An alternative would be to intubate him."

"Wait a sec." Shaun thought fast. "Can you hold off on the intubation? Surely BiPAP is less intrusive." The thought of his dad with a tube down his throat…

"Both will feel foreign and will irritate him, and restrict his movement," Doctor Sharma informed him. "The fact that he didn't resist the BiPAP mask is an indication of just how sick he is."

Oh God.

Nathan reached into his bag, removed a plastic wallet, and handed it to Shaun. "This is a copy of your dad's healthcare proxy. You might wanna look at this before making any decisions."

"Your father has a living will in place?" the doctor asked. Shaun nodded. "Okay. Our first move is to attempt to make him better."

"Pneumonia doesn't have to be lethal, does it? He could improve?" Except in Shaun's head a battle had started as he tried to weigh length of life versus quality of life. God knew he didn't want to lose Dad just yet, but if he was going to be in distress…

"Let's see how he responds to treatment before

we make any decisions," Doctor Sharma murmured.

"This isn't easy, I know." Nathan's voice was quiet. "Your dad chose a hospice, should the need arise, but like the doc says, let's wait and see."

Shaun straightened. "I knew it was coming, but I guess I wasn't ready for it to be this soon." He glanced at Nathan. His throat seized, and tears pricked his eyes. All he wanted was a hug. With an effort, he got himself under control, and gave the doc his attention. "Can I see him?"

"We're getting him a bed in ICU where we can properly monitor his condition."

"He… he's critical?" Even the acronym made his heart sink.

"Peter needs to be in a critical care bed," Doctor Sharma said in a gentle but firm tone. "I'll see to that now." He patted Shaun's arm, then left the waiting room.

Shaun dropped into the chair like a stone, and Nathan knelt in front of him. "Can I get you anything? Some water? Coffee?"

"Coffee would be good. I… I'm gonna call the restaurant, let 'em know what's going on."

Nathan patted his arm, stood, and went in search of coffee.

Shaun put his head in his hands. *Please, God, don't let him be in pain. Don't let him suffer.*

"Shaun?"

He jerked his head up at the familiar voice. Teresa Cyr was walking toward him, dressed in blue scrubs. Shaun stood. "Hey, Teresa." He hadn't seen her since the wedding in April.

"I was in the Emergency Room when your dad came in." She gave him a hug.

"They think it's aspiration pneumonia." He'd forgotten she was a nurse.

Her face fell. "Aw, bummer. Have you told any of the others? Finn? Levi?"

"Not yet. I only just found out myself. I was gonna call after I talk with my boss."

She cocked her head to one side. "Want me to call one of the boys? I can do that, as long as you're okay with it. I've got Finn's number, and Levi's."

He shuddered out a sigh. "Thanks. You can call either of them." He knew once one of them heard the news, word would get around.

"Are you here on your own?"

Shaun shook his head. "Dad's nurse, Nathan, is with me. He's just gone to get me some coffee."

"Okay, as long as you have someone." Teresa squeezed his upper arm. "If you need me—for *anything*—go to the nurses' station and ask for me, all right? I'll stop by later and see how he's doing."

"Thanks, Teresa."

She gave him another hug, and his throat grew tight. "Hang in there, okay?" Then she released him, turned, and headed out of the room.

Shaun sat once more, his stomach clenched.

All he could do was wait.

Chapter Eleven

It wasn't until late evening that Nathan dragged his thoughts away from the present situation, and remembered there was a furball that needed feeding. Nathan should have been home hours ago, and by now Cat had probably pissed in all his shoes, shredded his clothes, and taken a dump in the middle of the rug.

I don't want to leave Shaun.

He gazed at Shaun's drawn face, the brow that was furrowed even as he grabbed a few minutes of shuteye. It had taken Nathan all afternoon and most of the evening to convince him to close his eyes, for Christ's sake. ICU was quiet, except for the *hum* and *whir* of machinery and breathing apparatus. Peter was one of only three patients.

Peter had been asleep most of the day. The nurses had been in and out, checking him regularly, and adding antibiotics to his IV. The BiPAP mask was in place, but Nathan knew the next step would be intubation if there was no improvement after twenty-four to forty-eight hours.

The door to ICU opened, and a nurse came in. Judging by her scrubs, she worked in the Emergency Room. She peered at Shaun, then beckoned for Nathan to step outside. Nathan got out of his chair as quietly as he could, crept around the bed, and followed her out of the room.

Once outside, he glanced at her name badge. "Is there something I can do for you, Nurse Cyr?"

She held out her hand. "Call me Teresa. I'm a friend of Shaun's. You were with his dad when they brought him in this morning."

They shook. "I'm Nathan Simpson, Peter's nurse. I've been taking care of him since May."

She regarded him for a moment. "Do you know a Macy Dennis?"

He blinked. "Sure. I worked with her. We were in ICU." Macy had been one of his cheerleaders.

Teresa smiled. "She was my mentor when I was training. She talked about you."

"Uh-oh." He wiped his forehead.

She laughed. "You're good. She liked your attitude."

Nathan wondered for a moment how she'd put two and two together, then realized it was more a case of adding his name, occupation and appearance. *There can't be that many Black male nurses in Maine, right?*

Teresa inclined her head toward the room. "I've been in the ER all day, but I'm off duty now. I wanted to stop by and see how his dad is doing." Her face tightened. "Shaun has had such a shit deal. First his mom…" She stared through the glass to where Shaun dozed in his chair. "Can you get him to go home and get some sleep?"

"Believe me, I've been trying." Nathan rubbed his cheek. He needed some sleep too. He was beyond tired.

Teresa gave him a warm glance. "Want me to bring you both some coffee? Or hot chocolate? I can do that before I head home."

He smiled. "That's really kind. Thank you. Hot chocolate might be better."

"No problem. I'll be right back." She patted his

arm, then turned and strode briskly along the hallway.

Nathan let himself back into the ICU with the code the nurse had given him. Shaun started, then jerked his head toward Peter in obvious panic.

"It's okay," Nathan assured him. "He's asleep."

Shaun gazed at the heart monitor that recorded the blip of each heartbeat. "Is he the same?"

Nathan sighed. "Yeah. He's holding on." He wanted to tell Shaun Peter would improve, but his gut told him that would be false hope. "Look, there's nothing you can do for him right now. He's in the best hands. Why not go home and get some real sleep?"

"I had a nap," Shaun protested.

"You can't sleep here, there's too much noise. And they do have visiting hours, even in the ICU." Then the door opened, and Teresa walked in with a cardboard tray.

"Hey. Thought you might need this." She held out the insulated paper cups. "And there's someone outside who wants to see you. Unfortunately only two visitors per patient are allowed."

Nathan peered at the window. The visitor was a guy with black hair and a beard, about Shaun's age. It had to be one of his friends.

Shaun followed his gaze, and smiled. "Levi."

"I knew it wouldn't be long before one of them showed up." Teresa placed the other cup on the bedside table. "I've got to go now, but I'll stop by before I start my next shift, and see how he's doing."

Shaun stood and hugged her. "Thanks, Teresa."

"No problem." She gave Nathan a nod, then left the room. Levi stood by the window, his gaze fixed on Peter, his expression sad.

Nathan had recognized the name. "I'll step

outside while he visits." He grabbed his coat and walked to the door, but gestured to Levi to stay put. Once the door was closed, Nathan spoke quickly. "I'm Nathan, Peter's nurse. Shaun's spoken about you."

"Same here. He says you're great with his dad."

"You think you could do me a favor?"

Levi arched his eyebrows. "Okay…"

"What Shaun needs right now is to go home and sleep in his own bed, at least for a few hours. I don't think Peter will go into decline in that time, and Shaun's gonna need all his strength. The thing is… he's being stubborn. Maybe you can convince him."

"You think he'll listen to me?"

Nathan was certain of it. "I have to go home and feed my cat, but I'll be right back. And if you manage to get him to change his mind while I'm gone, I'll take him home and make sure he ends up in bed."

"I'd take him home myself, but I need to get back to my grandmother, and she's in the opposite direction. Are you sure you don't mind?"

"Not at all."

"Thanks." Levi smiled. "He's lucky to have you in his corner. Go feed your cat. I'll stay till you return."

"Thank you." Nathan hurried along the hallway.

Peter, don't make me a liar and take a turn for the worse while I'm gone, okay?

Shaun found himself enveloped in a tight hug. "I'm so glad to see you," he whispered.

"Teresa said he could only have a couple of visitors at a time," Levi said as he released him. "I won the toss." He removed his coat and hung it on the back of a chair. "I didn't bring flowers or balloons 'cause she said they're not allowed in here. Everyone sends their love."

Shaun pointed to his phone on the cabinet beside the bed. "I've had messages from all of them." Sweet messages. He chuckled. "Seb's was funny. He sent me a meme with two dogs in scrubs."

Levi grinned. "Yeah, I think a lot of us got that one."

Shaun retook his seat. "Where did Nathan go?"

"Home to feed his cat. He said he'll be right back though."

Shaun stared at him. "Oh my God. Cat must be starving." He reached for his phone. "I'll text Nathan and tell him he doesn't need to come back. He must be exhausted."

Levi bit his lip. "Like *you* are, you mean?"

He stilled. "It shows, huh?"

Levi stood next to Shaun, his hand on Shaun's shoulder. "Listen to me, please. You're no good to your dad if you're running on fumes. Let Nathan take you home. Seems to me you could both use some sleep."

Shaun was too weary to fight. "Okay." He picked up the cup of hot chocolate and took a sip.

"That's it? No arguments?"

Shaun snorted. "Too damn tired to argue."

Levi squeezed his shoulder. "Good." He walked around the bed and sat in the other chair, gazing at Shaun's dad. "Does he know you're here?"

Shaun had no idea. "There hasn't been much out of him since they brought him to ICU."

"If you need *anything*, you only have to ask, you know that?"

Shaun smiled. "I know. And thanks." He looked at his dad. "I looked up BiPAP online. It said it can't be continued for more than twenty-four to forty-eight hours without a break. Otherwise it causes problems." He glanced at Levi. "I'm not stupid. If the antibiotics and the BiPAP don't help, they'll intubate him. I just know he'd hate that. And if he gets worse…"

"What happens then?" Levi asked in a soft voice.

He swallowed. "Dad picked out a hospice, not far from here actually. He'll be transferred there."

"But you'll be the one who gets to decide that?"

Shaun nodded. "Jesus, this stinks."

Levi covered his dad's hand with his own. "I know it's not something you want to think about, but you have to do what's best for him. I know I'm going to be faced with the same situation one day. I mean, Grammy's only seventy, but…" He took a deep breath. "She's already told me she's named me as her healthcare proxy." His eyes met Shaun's. "And I'm not ready to lose her either."

Shaun took his dad's other hand, careful of the wires and tubes. "There are things I meant to tell him. Things I should have told him years ago." One thing in particular.

"I'm sure he'll hear you, if you talk to him," Levi urged. "Don't they say you should talk to patients as if they can hear and understand every word? And there's always the chance he *will* hear you. Maybe you should tell him now, rather than wait a while."

"Maybe." Shaun listened to the rhythmic sounds of his dad's breathing as the BiPAP delivered airway pressure to aid both inhalation and exhalation.

Levi cleared his throat. "About Nathan…"

"What about him?"

"You don't think there's something you maybe should've told us about him?"

"Such as?" As if Shaun couldn't guess.

Levi rolled his eyes. "Oh, I don't know. Maybe the fact that he's *hot?*"

What the fuck? "Levi!" Shaun blurted. The nurse on the other side of the room raised her eyebrows, her lips twitching. Then she placed a finger to her lips. "Hey, keep the noise down," Shaun whispered to Levi.

"Oopsie. Sorry." Levi leaned closer, his voice low. "You telling me you haven't noticed? What planet are you on, dude? I mean, I'm not into older guys, but for him, I'd be sorely tempted to see what all the fuss was about."

For a moment, Shaun couldn't believe what he was hearing, but then the light dawned. "I get it. You're trying to take my mind off Dad."

Levi blinked. "Well… yeah… but that doesn't make Nathan any less hot. Seb would be drooling." He stared at Shaun. "Oh, come *on.*"

"Okay, okay, he's good-looking, all right?" He shook his head. "How did you know?"

"Know what?"

"That he's gay."

Levi's mouth fell open. "He is? I had no idea." He grinned. "Even better."

"Can we not talk about this right now? And what does it matter if he's gay or straight?"

"It doesn't." Levi smiled. "I'm just checking that you noticed what a hot-looking man he is." He stood. "Sorry. I need to find a restroom. Be right back." He headed for the door.

Shaun scanned the ICU. There were no other visitors, and the nurse was standing by a bed, writing on a chart.

No time like the present.

He held Dad's hand between his. "Hey, Dad? I don't know if you can hear me, but… there's something I think you should know. I meant to tell you and Mom ages ago, but…" He inhaled deeply. "Dad, I… I'm gay. I've known it since I was maybe seventeen. And I promised myself one day I'd sit you and Mom down, and I'd tell you." He bit his lip. "Guess you already know how *that* went. I don't know why I never brought it up. I was sure, deep down, you wouldn't have a problem with me liking guys—you *or* Mom. There just seemed to be so many other things that were more important, and I put it off, and put it off, and…" He squeezed his dad's hand. "I know what you'd be asking me, if you could. You'd wanna know if there's someone special. Well… there is… but it's not gonna come to anything, and I'm okay with that." Well, sort of okay. "And I think part of me knows I'm telling you all this now just to make *me* feel better, and yeah, that's selfish of me, but all the same, I hope you hear it."

Dad stirred. He locked gazes with Shaun. "Love you." The words were audible, despite the mask.

In that second Shaun knew with every bone in his body that his words had gotten through. He wiped away the hot tears that trickled down his face. "Love you too, Dad."

Dad closed his eyes, and Shaun held his breath.

Dad's chest rose and fell, and Shaun breathed again.
Not yet, Dad. Not yet.

Chapter Twelve

December 2

Shaun gazed at his dad. The BiPAP mask was gone, and in its place was a tube under his nose, delivering oxygen. There were no monitors in the quiet room, and gone were the familiar hospital noises. The hospice was a peaceful place. They'd transferred his dad that afternoon.

Shaun wasn't sure Dad had a clue about the move. He'd been unresponsive for the last twenty-four hours.

"How much longer can he stay like this?" he murmured, stroking Dad's hand.

"Could be a couple of days, three or four maybe." Nathan was looking at Dad's chart. "He's on morphine now. That will make him more comfortable."

Shaun's stomach clenched. "The morphine isn't there to help him… die faster, is it?"

Nathan shook his head. "Not at all. It's easing the work of breathing, and making his… transition peaceful."

"'Transition'. That's a better word." He gave Nathan the best smile he could muster. "Thanks for being with me while they moved him. I'm sure you have places to be." *But I'm grateful you stayed.*

"As of Monday, I'm officially on vacation for two weeks. I haven't taken one of those in a while. Then I'll work a couple of weeks before I take a few days off at Christmas."

"Will they assign you a new patient right away?" Shaun didn't want to think about Nathan not being around anymore.

"I've asked my boss to send me as part of a team. That way, two of us go to someone's home a couple of times a day, to wash and feed them. That means working less hours during the day."

The door opened, and a nurse came in. She gave Shaun a warm smile. "You can stay as long as you like, but we do encourage you to get some sleep if you can." She checked his dad's IV.

"What if..." Shaun swallowed. "What if he... goes while I'm not here?"

She regarded him with kind eyes. "I know you want to be here for him, but there's something you need to consider." She paused. "Your dad may not *want* you to watch him transition. We have no idea how aware he is right now, but..." Another pause. "We'd call you to let you know once he goes, to ask if you wanted to come in one last time." She walked around the bed and headed for the door. "I'll leave you to think about it."

When the door closed, Shaun put his head in his hands. "This is awful."

"It seems that way because you're bone-tired," Nathan said in a low voice. "Let me take you home."

"No."

Nathan sighed. "You must've only had two or three hours of sleep last night."

"And you know that, how?"

"Okay, so I was in the next room and I wasn't sleeping much either." Nathan got up from his chair and came around the bed to where Shaun sat. He laid his large hand on Shaun's shoulder. "Please... let me take care of you. That's what Peter would want."

It was on the tip of Shaun's tongue to say mentioning his dad was a pretty low trick, until he realized Nathan was right. *Dad wouldn't want to see me in such a mess.* And if his dad did see him...

"Okay. But... would you stay again?" He didn't want to be alone.

Nathan nodded. "Sure."

"Wait—what about Cat?"

Nathan waved his hand. "Already taken care of. He's staying with my upstairs neighbor. Which is probably where he spends most of his time anyway when I'm not home. I think as soon as I start the car engine, he's out of that kitty flap and zipping up the stairs to see his girlfriend."

"Cat has a girlfriend?"

He chuckled. "A Maine Coon by the name of Trixie. I should think she wears the pants—if you get my drift."

Shaun smiled. "Aw, that's nice. Cat's in love."

Nathan snorted. "I wouldn't go that far." He gestured to the bed. "Kiss your dad goodnight, and then I'll take you home."

Shaun stood, leaned over, and kissed Dad's forehead. "See you tomorrow," he whispered. As an afterthought—because what if this was the last time he'd get to say it?—he brought his lips to Dad's ear and whispered, "Love you, Dad."

When he straightened, Nathan was holding out his coat. "He knows," he murmured, his voice gentle.

Shaun hoped so.

As soon as they were through the front door, Nathan took charge.

"I'll find us something to eat. Then you can shower while I make the tea."

"I'm not all that hungry," Shaun confessed.

"You're still gonna eat, even if it's just a grilled cheese sandwich and a cup of soup." When Shaun's eyes lit up, he knew he'd hit pay dirt. "Do you have calls to make? Your phone was pinging like crazy when we left the hospice."

"Yeah, that was all the guys. I'll only call one of them. I'm too tired to cope with multiple conversations. Besides, I tell one, they all get to hear eventually." Shaun flopped onto the couch, and Nathan went through the arch into the kitchen.

It didn't take him long to rustle up some food, and by the time he called Shaun to eat, Nathan was seriously flagging. He glanced at Shaun as they sat. "All done?"

He nodded. "I called Dylan." He stared at the plates. "This looks really good." He sank onto a chair and his stomach growled. "Maybe I'm hungrier than I thought."

"Neither of us ate much today."

Shaun took a bite from his sandwich and the appreciative sounds that tumbled from his lips lightened Nathan's heart. "While I was on the phone to Dylan, something caught my eye."

"What was that?"

"You know the carved wooden box that sits on a shelf under the window?"

Nathan frowned. "Wait—the big one?"

Shaun nodded. "My mom's ashes are in there. Dad said when *he* went, I was to have him cremated too, then mix their ashes."

"And what did he ask you to do with them? Scatter them someplace special? Bury them?" Momma still had his dad's ashes. She said she hadn't come up with the perfect place for them yet.

Shaun sighed. "He said he was leaving that part up to me, because by then he'd be beyond caring—and he'd be with Mom."

"Sounds like they were a special couple."

"They were. They just didn't have long enough together, that's all."

They ate in silence for the rest of the meal, although Nathan put that down to fatigue rather than reflection. When they were done, he placed the dishes in the dishwasher. "I'll make tea, you go grab a shower. You'll feel better for it."

"Okay." Shaun got up from the table and trudged wearily toward his room. Nathan did a quick tidy-up, then put the kettle on. He took two peach tea bags from their box, dropped them into two cups, and leaned against the sink as he waited for the water to boil. By the sound of it, Shaun hadn't spent too long in the shower.

I hope I sleep more than I did last night. The guest bed was comfortable enough, but Nathan had been unable to get his mind to shut down.

He carried the cups to Shaun's room, and came to a halt in the doorway.

Shaun was lying on his side in his robe, fast asleep on top of the comforter.

Nathan put the cups down on the nightstand, then crept into the closet and removed a folded comforter from the high shelf. He spread it carefully over Shaun's still form, not wanting to wake him. Nathan turned off the beside lamp, and was on his way out of the room when Shaun let out a whimper.

Nathan returned to the bed, standing there in silence, waiting for Shaun's steady breathing to resume. When it didn't, Nathan let out a soft sigh, drew back the comforter, and lay down beside Shaun, curled around him. He covered them both, then put his arm around Shaun.

"I've got you," he whispered. "Go to sleep."

Within seconds, Shaun's breathing deepened and he relaxed in Nathan's arms. Nathan held him close, warmth radiating through the cotton robe.

Sleep, sweetheart.

A moment later, Nathan slipped into a warm, comforting slumber.

December 3

Nathan opened his eyes, and he caught his breath. Shaun was still in his arms, except at some point he'd rolled over and snuggled up to Nathan.

Damn, he feels good.

No sooner had the thought flitted through his

mind, than Nathan berated himself for it. It wasn't right. Peter was about to check out any minute, and yet here *he* was, lying warm and cozy, enjoying holding Shaun.

He extricated himself with extreme care, then crept out of the room. When the aroma of freshly brewed coffee filled the kitchen, he poured two cups and returned to the bedroom. Their tea was still on the nightstand, cold and forgotten.

Shaun's nose twitched, and he slowly opened his eyes. "Hey."

"Good morning." Nathan sat on the edge of the bed. "Feel better?" They'd slept more than seven hours. The first thing Nathan had done once he'd gotten Shaun's phone, was to check it for messages, but there were none.

Shaun stretched. "I had a wonderful dream. I was a kid again, maybe six or seven, and I'd fallen off my bicycle."

Nathan arched his eyebrows. "That doesn't sound so wonderful to me."

"Hey, let me finish." Shaun sat up in bed, reaching for his coffee cup. "Dad washed my knee, stuck a Band-aid on it, and carried me to my room. Then he lay down on the bed and held me all night." He swallowed. "It felt so... *real.* I knew I was safe and loved."

Nathan didn't trust himself to speak. He sipped his coffee.

Shaun glanced toward the bedroom door. "Has there been any news?"

He shook his head. "I'll make breakfast, then we'll go see your dad. Unless you want to be alone with him?" Nathan was fine with that.

Shaun blinked. "Would you come with me? I want you to be there too. Besides…" His sad smile tore at Nathan's insides. "I've told him everything I needed to."

"Sure."

Dear Lord, the irony. A few days ago, he'd left Shaun with Levi, praying Peter didn't decide to check out while he'd been gone. Now?

He was praying Peter didn't linger. He didn't think Shaun could take much more.

December 6

"Whassup? What time is it?" Shaun struggled to wake up. A click followed, and lamplight flooded his room. Nathan stood beside the bed in his robe, his face grave as he held out Shaun's phone.

Just like that, Shaun knew.

He took it. "Shaun Clark here."

"Mr. Clark, it's Nurse Michaels from Kindred hospice here. Your father passed about ten minutes ago. He went peacefully in his sleep. Our deepest condolences. If you'd like to come in to say goodbye, that would be okay."

Shaun hadn't expected the feeling of numbness that stole over him. "Thank you for calling. I'll be there." He disconnected.

"I'll take you." Nathan removed the phone from his grasp.

"Thanks." There was something stuck in his throat that wouldn't budge, and his eyes felt dry and achy. Shaun threw back the comforter and swung his legs out of bed.

He's really gone.

"It feels as if you're stuck in this thick mental fog, doesn't it?"

Shaun gazed at him. "Yes. How did you—"

"We lost my dad a few years back. Saying goodbye… it gives you a chance to see him at peace. Because he is. I believe that."

Shaun managed a smile. "Of course he is. He's with Mom." And then the dam broke. He struggled to draw breath as the tears fell, and Nathan sat beside him, his arm around Shaun's shoulders.

"Let it out," he murmured. "It's okay to cry."

It was as if Shaun had been waiting for permission to sob his heart out. He buried his face in Nathan's robe, threw his arms around Nathan's neck, and clung to him until the tears ebbed away. Nathan held him through it all, offering no words, nothing but the gentle movement of his hands on Shaun's back, but it was enough.

When he had himself under control once more, Shaun let go of Nathan and wiped his eyes. "Thanks for staying. Cat must think he's been abandoned."

Nathan's eyes glistened too. "*He's* fine—right now I'm more concerned about you." He stroked Shaun's hair. "Come on. Let's get dressed."

Shaun could manage that. He could do anything that kept his thoughts from that quiet room where his dad lay, having finally escaped the confusion and frustration that had plagued him for so many years.

God, you take care of them both, okay?

He took a couple of deep breaths, then reached for his clothes.

Time to say goodbye.

The nurse held the door for them, and Shaun walked into the room, Nathan following. Dad lay in bed beneath a pale blue blanket, his oxygen tube gone, his head supported by thick pillows.

Shaun's breathing hitched. "He looks as if he's asleep." He couldn't remember the last time Dad had looked so rested.

"I'll leave you alone," the nurse murmured, pulling the door closed behind her as she retreated.

Shaun stepped closer. "I thought he'd look…different somehow. Mom did, a little, when I saw her in her casket."

"Yeah, but that was after they'd gotten her ready. You've been with your dad every day since he got sick. And this has been a peaceful passing."

The reminder eased Shaun's aching heart a little. "You're right. He's at peace."

"Finally." Nathan's voice cracked. When Shaun turned to gaze at him, Nathan waved his hand. "Never you mind about me. I've lost so many patients, you'd think I'd be used to it by now, but your dad…"

"You cared for him, didn't you?" Shaun's eyes grew hot. "As a person, I mean, not as a patient."

"Yeah, I did."

Shaun brought his attention back to the bed. "You waited till I was out of the room, didn't you, Dad?" He leaned over and pressed his lips to his dad's forehead as he'd done hours before. Except this time was different, and he knew it.

Dad wasn't there anymore.

"Goodbye, Dad. Give my love to Mom." A single tear burst like a star on his dad's brow, and Shaun straightened, wiping his eyes. "Thought I was all cried out."

"You'll never be that," Nathan told him. "Years from now, something will come to mind about him, and you'll cry again, and again, and again. He'll never be out of your life, because he's in your heart."

"God, yes." Shaun spun around to find Nathan's tall frame blocking his way, and he didn't hesitate. He pressed his face against Nathan's chest and wept.

"I've got you," Nathan murmured. "I've got you. And the Lord has your dad in his safekeeping."

Shaun closed his eyes and breathed in Nathan's strength, his smell, the touch of his hands on Shaun's back...

Thank you, God, for Nathan.

Chapter Thirteen

December 9

One thought had crossed Shaun's mind constantly in the days since Dad passed: dying was a real ball ache. There was so much to do. Kudos to Dad, he'd made a lot of arrangements, but each day added something else to Shaun's to-do list.

Thank God for Nathan. That thought had crossed his mind on several occasions too. Nathan had been through this process when his dad died, and he'd helped his mom. It was as if he had a mental list and was checking it off.

Nathan and Dad were pretty similar, when Shaun thought about it. Dad had made what he called a Grim Reaper file, containing all the information Shaun would need. He'd first mentioned it a few years ago, and Shaun hadn't paid all that much attention—he hadn't wanted to think about losing Dad. But when he'd found the plastic folder in his dad's desk, the opening page had brought fresh tears to his eyes. He could hear his dad saying every word, as if he was there in the room.

Shaun,

I saw this in a movie once, and I thought at the time what a great idea. One place for all the info you'll need. At least, I hope *it's all the info—I might have forgotten one or two things—but I'm sure David Brennan will help if he can. He's my lawyer, and you'll find his number in here. Call him once you've read this, if you haven't already.*

About my funeral… It's already paid for—that's one less thing you need to think about. I've even chosen the music. No, I'm not telling you what I've picked, you'll have to wait and see. I've made a few lists for you that I hope will make things a little easier. You'll find the names of people you'll need to call to invite to see me off, assuming they're still breathing, of course. I can't do that from where I am. (Joke) I left you out of so much when your mom died—you were still in school, and that was enough for you to cope with. But now this falls to you.

One thing that's included in my funeral plan is the catering for after. Call it a celebration of my life. All you have to do is invite the guests.

I know you'll do me proud, son.
Love you.

Dad.

Shaun had re-read the letter three or four times, just to hear his dad's voice inside his head once more. The list of names contained some he didn't recognize, but thankfully Dad had written phone numbers next to each one.

The doorbell rang, snapping him back into the moment. *Is it Nathan time already?* Shaun opened the door to find him standing there, rubbing his arms briskly. "Cold enough for you?" His phone had showed it was twenty-five degrees out. He smiled. "Good morning. Coffee's on and I've got a fire going." He glanced down at the pet carrier in Nathan's hand. "Aw, you did as I asked."

Nathan chuckled. "I still think you're crazy. Now Cat'll piss in *your* shoes instead." As Shaun closed the door, Nathan set down the carrier and opened the cage door. The short-haired tabby kitty poked his head out to peer at his surroundings, then scooted across the wooden floor to the fireplace. His nose twitched as he watched the flames licking the logs. "Cat..." Nathan's voice was firm.

Shaun snickered. "Does he ever pay attention to what you say?"

"Never." Then Shaun breathed easier as Cat turned three times before settling on the rug. Nathan let out a wry chuckle. "Trust Cat to pick out the warmest spot." He reached into the carrier. "I brought his bowls and some food, but I don't think he'll move from that spot all day." Even as he spoke, Cat closed his eyes, his tail overlapping his paws. "The litterbox is in the car. I'll bring it in in a sec."

"Let's leave him to his snooze." Shaun headed for the kitchen. "He'll be okay, won't he?"

"He's already asleep. When I go, I'm coming back as a cat." Nathan placed the bowls on the floor in a corner, then sat at the kitchen table. "What's on today's list?"

Shaun poured the coffee. "We've gotten so much done already. And I do mean we—you've been awesome. I've leaned on you a lot the last few days."

"You lean all you want. That's why I'm here." Nathan's lips twitched. "Although... your dad's lawyer seemed pretty confused to see me here."

"He can be as confused as he likes. You're a godsend." Nathan had visited every day, and Shaun looked forward to seeing him. It was more than the help and support Nathan offered—it was the man himself. *I really like having him around.* Except he knew once Nathan went back to work, Shaun would be relegated to the list of Nathan's previous clients. The realization only served to exacerbate Shaun's aching heart.

I've come to rely on him. To trust him. To... Shaun couldn't quantify all his emotions when it came to Nathan. It felt like more than just friendship, at least, it did from Shaun's perspective.

Shaun placed the cups on the table, then reached for his notepad, scanning his list. "Dad's obituary is with the funeral home—they're posting it online—and I've sent it to the local newspaper. I've called Dad's insurance company, the disability department, the funeral home..."

"Are you still sure you don't wanna say something at the service?"

Shaun sighed. "I don't think I could manage that. I've given the celebrant as much information about Dad as I could. Dad didn't want a long service, just the opportunity for people to say their goodbyes."

"Have you contacted everyone on his list?"

Shaun nodded. "Dad was an only child, but he sure had a lot of cousins. Some of them I've never seen."

"What about your friends?"

He smiled. "They're all coming, partners too." Shaun shook his head. "Partners... We were all single guys this time last year."

Nathan cocked his head to one side. "Have you read it yet?"

Shaun didn't need to ask what *it* referred to. David Brennan had brought a sealed envelope with him, on which was written in Dad's precise hand, *To be given to Shaun when I'm gone.*

He hadn't gotten up enough nerve to open it.

"You haven't, have you?"

"No. Maybe because that will bring it home to me that he's truly gone." Shaun gestured to the kitchen. "It doesn't matter if Dad left me this place—it still feels like his house. This morning, I went into his closet. I touched the clothes that still smelled of him. There was his favorite Christmas sweater, the one Mom knitted for him." He chuckled. "It has the goofiest reindeer you've ever seen. Knitting wasn't one of her strengths, but Dad kept it and wore it every year. Then I found his heavy winter coat, so thick and warm. I think it was from when he was younger, but he'd kept it. Put it this way—it fits me."

"Will you wear it?"

"Yeah. I might even wear it on Friday at the funeral."

"He'd like that."

Shaun sipped his coffee. "He had this one drawer full of odd socks. He said Mom used to swear the dryer ate the missing ones. Or she'd joke that for every sock he lost, she gained a plastic lid for a container that wasn't in her kitchen cabinets."

Nathan reached across the table and covered Shaun's hand. "Shaun... read the letter. If your dad went to the trouble of writing one, it must have been important to him." Nathan's hand engulfed his.

He knew Nathan was right. "Okay, I'll read it. But then we need to talk about his clothes. I'm gonna need your help bagging them all up for Goodwill."

"Read first—talk after." Nathan withdrew his hand and folded his arms.

"Did my dad ever call you bossy?"

Nathan smiled. "All the time. Now read the letter."

Shaun got up and walked into the living room,

where the folder sat on the table next to Dad's chair. *And that's something else to add to my list.* He picked up the folder and returned to the kitchen, passing Cat who was still curled up by the fire.

Nathan's right. Cats have the best life.

"I've been thinking," he said as he retook his seat. "Dad's recliner…"

"What about it?"

"I think I'll donate it to the hospice. They might find a good home for it, or keep it there."

"I like that idea. Give them a call—*after* you've read the—"

"Okay, okay!" Shaun rolled his eyes.

Nathan held up his hands. "Man, you're just like your dad. He could've won gold medals in prevarication."

Shaun didn't mind that comparison in the slightest.

He removed the long cream envelope from the folder. "Here goes…" He tore the end off, and took out the single sheet of paper. His hands shook a little as he unfolded it. The letter was dated two years previous.

Shaun,

If you're reading this, then I'm not around anymore. I thought long and hard about what I wanted to say to you, and most of it is stuff I should have said when I was alive. So either I did tell you, and then forgot to tell David Brennan to tear this up, or I didn't, and for that I'm sorry. I'm writing it now because today I woke up with a clear mind, something I took for granted when I was your age. Little did I know, huh? So I'm taking advantage of a few moments of clarity to share some things with you.

I have to say, it feels weird writing about this stuff,

knowing I won't be around when you read it. And yeah, I'm tearing up a little as I write. No one wants to think about checking out, but I had to do this.

You're a wonderful son. Don't ever think otherwise. You were my rock when your mom passed, and you've been my rock ever since. But... that support came at a cost, one I'm acutely aware of.

You put your life on hold for me.

I know you said you wanted to start earning rather than go to college, but I reckon that was a lie. I think you chose to follow that path because you didn't want to be far from me. Was it obvious even then, this disease that has ravaged my brain? Were there signs before the diagnosis? Maybe, to you. Maybe even to your mom, when I think back on it.

But you don't have to follow that path anymore, not if you don't want to. I've made sure of that. I've left you well provided for. The house is yours, to do with as you please. And with all those policies I took out when you were born, there should be enough money for you to go back to school—if that's what you want.

Hopefully, I'm giving you options. A different future. You don't have to do anything right away. Take time to think. If you want to stay a server in that restaurant, that's absolutely fine. But if you don't...

You've been focused on me for the past seven years.

It's time to focus on Shaun Clark. Time for you to find some happiness.

Love you, son.

Your Dad.

"Oh God." Shaun put down the letter, for fear his tears would blur his dad's penmanship. "I didn't fool him for an instant."

Nathan was out of his seat and beside Shaun in a heartbeat. He bent low and put his arm around Shaun's shoulders. Shaun threw his arms around Nathan, burying his face in Nathan's warmth. A gentle hand stroked his hair. He didn't say the grief would pass, nor did he say the pain would lessen. Without words, he somehow let Shaun know the one thing that mattered right then.

He was there for Shaun.

"I'm okay." Shaun pulled back and wiped his eyes.

"No, you're not, but it's only been three days." Nathan sat. "And we've talked about this. You cry any time you feel like it."

Shaun picked up the sheet of paper. "You can read this. I don't think anything in it will come as any great surprise. You spent a lot of time with my dad."

Nathan took it and read it in silence. When he was done, he lowered the letter to the table with a heavy sigh. "Your dad…" He paused. "Will you keep the house?"

"Why not? I wouldn't want to go through the horrors of moving. Don't they say it's one of the most stressful things there is? And this house has no bad memories for me. It might take a while till it feels as if it's *my* house, but I'm okay with that."

"He made some good points. And he's right. Take time to figure out what you want to do with your life."

Shaun couldn't think about that now, not when there was still the funeral to come. "I'll miss you after this weekend." He managed a smile. "I've gotten used to you being around."

"I'm not gonna disappear, just because I go

back to work. You don't get rid of me that easily."

They were the best words Shaun had heard in a while.

Chapter Fourteen

December 11

Shaun waited for the car that was to take him to the funeral home. He'd opted not to see his dad before they closed the casket. He wanted to remember him as he'd been, before the mortuary got to work on him.

The house felt so still. Even the street outside was quiet.

Then the doorbell shattered the silence. Shaun gave Nathan a warm smile as he crossed the threshold. "You look nice."

Nathan glanced at his suit. "I'd say make the most of it, because I only ever wear a suit on two occasions—weddings and funerals." His eyes brightened when he caught sight of the floral arrangement standing on Dad's table. "Aw, they got here. I'll let Momma know."

"Thanks. And please thank her for me. I wanted to do that, but I don't have her number." The beautiful flowers had arrived the previous day, along with a card that had made him tear up.

"I'd ask if you're ready for this, but that's a stupid question."

Shaun took a bold step. "You know what I really need right now?"

"What?"

He swallowed. "A hug."

Nathan smiled. "I got plenty to go around." He held his arms wide, and Shaun stepped into them, wrapping his arms around Nathan. He felt surrounded by strength, and for a moment he was transported back to that dream, the one about his dad and a fall off his bicycle. Nathan was warm, and he smelled…

Good. He smells good.

"Better?" Nathan murmured.

Shaun nodded, unwilling to talk. Anything to hold onto the welcome feeling of security.

"Are you sure about me going in the car with you?"

Shaun let him go and took a step back. "Yeah, I'm sure. I don't wanna be on my own. And we're both going to the same place. This way, someone else gets to drive." He cocked his head. "Is that okay?"

Nathan smiled. "Sure. If there was no car, I'd take you there myself." He inclined his head toward the window. "And speaking of cars… It's time."

Shaun caught a glimpse of gleaming black and polished chrome outside, standing out against the white blanket of snow that coated everything in sight. "You're right. Let's go say goodbye to Dad." All morning, it had felt as if his emotions were held tightly in place by a wire mesh that bit gently into his flesh. Maybe the funeral would be the release he needed.

Maybe.

Organ music played low in the background as they walked into the room where the service would be held. The soft perfume of flowers filled the air. At the front was the coffin, placed between floral arrangements, and a lectern stood to the side. White lilies and red roses covered the coffin, and Nathan knew the roses were for Shaun's mom. They had been her favorite flower.

Chairs had been set out in two blocks, with a center aisle, and Nathan saw many of the front rows on the left were already occupied. Shaun had said the funeral director had reserved seats for Dad's family and Shaun's friends. Levi stood as they approached, and Shaun was on the receiving end of a fierce hug.

When Levi released him, Nathan touched Shaun's arm lightly. "I'll go find a seat. You need to sit with your friends." They took up the first three rows, and Nathan was aware of their scrutiny. Before Shaun could reply, a couple of them stood and came over to hug him.

Levi frowned. "We've saved you the seat next to Shaun."

Nathan shook his head. "Thank you, but that's for family, and that means all of you."

Levi arched his eyebrows. "Newsflash for you, Nathan. You're family now." He smiled. "I'll do the introductions later at Shaun's house."

Nathan bit his lip as he surveyed the glances full of obvious curiosity. "Introductions—or interrogations?"

He chuckled. "Relax. They don't bite. Okay, Seb might give you a nibble, but his boyfriend will rein him in quickly." Levi held out his hand. "I'm glad you came."

Nathan shook it. "Peter was a wonderful man. I had to be here to pay my respects."

"I know Shaun appreciates that." Right then, the celebrant went to speak with Shaun, and soon everyone took their seats. Shaun sat in the middle of the front row, and Nathan took the empty chair next to his. When Shaun reached for Nathan's hand, Nathan didn't hesitate. He curled his fingers around Shaun's and leaned in.

"I've got you," Nathan murmured.

Shaun's gaze flickered in his direction, and he mouthed *Thank you*. Then he stilled when the organ music came to an end, and Bette Midler's soulful rendition of *Wind Beneath My Wings* poured out of the speakers as the celebrant took his place behind the lectern.

"Oh Dad." Shaun's eyes glistened. "This was from their favorite movie. Dad took her to see it the year they met. Mom used to sing it around the house."

Nathan tightened his grip on Shaun's hand while the celebrant spoke, not that Nathan was listening all that carefully: his attention was on Shaun. True to Peter's wishes, it was a short service, peppered with laughter here and there as the celebrant shared stories about Peter. At the end, those gathered were invited to say goodbye as they left.

The music began once more, and Shaun gaped at the opening lyrics of *Always Look on the Bright Side of Life* before bursting into laughter. "No wonder he didn't tell me what he'd chosen." He shook his head, wiping his eyes.

Nathan glanced around him at the smiling faces of the mourners. "Peter, you did good," he murmured. Then everyone stood, and silently filed past the coffin.

Shaun paused next to it, and laid his hand on the varnished surface. He didn't speak, but his Adam's apple bobbed. Then he gazed at Nathan, expelling a long breath.

Nathan laid his hand on Shaun's shoulder. "Let's get you home."

"You're staying for the reception, aren't you?"

He smiled. "Just you try and stop me."

Nathan kept a close eye on Shaun as he circulated through the packed living room. Not all the mourners had come back to the house: Shaun's friends were there, along with an elderly lady, and a few others. The lady was one of the first to approach him, her hand extended.

"Hello there. I'm Linda Brown, Levi's grandmother, but everyone calls me Grammy. You must be Nathan."

They shook. "Guilty as charged."

She peered up at him. "Lord, Shaun must get a crick in his neck every time you two talk." She smiled. "I've known him since he was seventeen." Her eyes twinkled. "Levi says you're a good man."

"Levi is very kind. He only met me once before today."

Grammy waved her hand. "He's a good judge of character. Now, on to important matters. You're invited to my New Year's party."

He stilled. "Ma'am, you don't even know me."

She blinked. "Shaun trusts you. That's all I need to know. And I'm not such a bad judge of character myself." Grammy reached up and patted his cheek. "Besides, it's Shaun's birthday, so it'll be a double celebration this year."

He frowned. "*This* year?"

Grammy looked to where Shaun stood with an older man, both deep in discussion, and Nathan's throat tightened to see the fondness in her glance. "Birthdays have kinda passed him by. Not much of a surprise, huh? But this year, I'm gonna bake him a cake, *and* I'll stick all twenty-seven candles in it."

A young man walked up to them. "Grammy, I got you a glass of port. I know you like it." He grinned. "And seeing as Levi's doing the driving, you can drink as much as you like." He wagged his finger. "Just no getting falling-down drunk. I know what you're like."

"You little article." Grammy took the proffered glass. "You're not too old to be spanked, y'know." That twinkle was back. "Maybe I should suggest it to Wade." Then she gave Nathan a nod, and walked off toward where Levi stood with three of the friends.

The guy held out his hand. "I'm Ben. And you're Nathan the nurse."

Nathan shook. "That's me, but just Nathan will do."

"Okay, Just Nathan…" Ben inclined his head toward Grammy. "She's awesome."

"I'm thinking formidable too."

Ben cackled. "Oh yeah." His expression grew serious. "Levi said you took great care of Shaun's dad. And I know you've been there for Shaun since he passed. Thank you. Shaun's a sweet guy. He needs someone to lean on right now." He aimed a frank stare at Nathan. "So… a little bird tells me you're gay."

Nathan was glad he wasn't drinking. "Wow. I think I just got whiplash from the change in direction. You don't have a filter, do you?"

"'A filter'? What's that?" Ben's eyes danced with amusement.

"Can I ask which little bird?"

"That's easy. Shaun told Levi, and then Levi told everyone else. Are you single?"

Nathan could give as good as he got. "Why, are you interested?" he quipped. Then he wondered how the subject of his sexuality had come up in conversation. *Shaun was talking about me?*

Ben grinned. "Nope." He gestured to a guy who was the epitome of tall, dark and handsome. "That's my boyfriend, Wade. He's about as much as I can handle." There was an evil glint in his eyes. "But if I *was* to be tempted, you'd fit the bill. I like 'em big, and dear *Lord*, you're big."

"You noticed, huh?" Nathan liked Ben's incorrigibility.

"Couldn't miss ya. But maybe you already have your eye on someone."

"Excuse me?"

Ben shrugged. "I see a lot. And while *I'm* not in the market for a guy, someone else I know is. You wanna know what I think?"

Nathan chuckled. "I have a feeling you're gonna tell me anyway."

"You got that right. And you should totally go for it."

Nathan frowned. "You just lost me. Go for what?"

Ben leaned in, his voice barely more than a murmur. "Shaun's more of a *who* than a *what*, but I don't think he'd say no. But hey, you won't know until you ask, right? And now I think I need a drink." That grin was still evident. "Wade's driving, after all." He ambled off toward the kitchen.

Nathan stared after him. Either he was going crazy, or Ben had just suggested Shaun might be interested in guys. To be specific, in him.

In me? Either Shaun was really good at keeping secrets, or Nathan was lousy at picking up on clues.

Are we nearly there yet?

The day was taking its toll, and while Shaun's heart felt a little lighter, he was weary. He'd thanked everyone who'd come to pay their respects, not that he'd known some of them. Dad's cousin Jerry was regaling him with stories about the things Dad had gotten up to when he was a kid. Some of it he'd heard before, but what made him smile was the obvious affection in Jerry's voice.

"Actually, I brought something with me that I wanted you to have. You know your mom and dad didn't meet until they were in their mid to late twenties, don't you?"

Shaun nodded. "Mom was twenty-four and Dad was twenty-nine."

"Well, they wanted to start work on a family

right away, but it didn't happen. A couple of years went by, and no babies. I don't know if they got medical help or something, but in '93, they announced Laura was pregnant. Your dad was so excited. And 1993 came to be known as the year of the late Christmas cards."

Shaun frowned. "I haven't heard any of this."

Jerry smiled. "The cards didn't arrive until after New Year's, and it was all your fault."

"Mine?"

He chuckled. "Sure. Laura had been due on December 18, and they were going to have a photo taken for the cards, of them with their new baby. Except you were late. You didn't put in an appearance until December 31. So all the cards went out late." Jerry smiled. "They waited for you." He turned to his wife. "Honey, you got that envelope?" She reached into her purse and removed a red envelope. Jerry held it out to Shaun. "I thought you might like this."

Shaun eased the card out of the envelope, and his throat seized. In the photo on the front, his mom and dad sat in front of a Christmas tree, Shaun cradled in Mom's arms, and both of them grinning. Happiness radiated from them.

"Have you seen this before?" Jerry asked him.

Shaun shook his head. "I had no idea. Thank you so much."

"You're welcome. And thank you for inviting us. I spent a lot of time with your dad when we were growing up. I'm glad he's at peace now."

Shaun couldn't talk anymore.

"Shaun, have you got a minute?" Nathan stood beside him. "They need you in the kitchen."

He swallowed. "Sure." He held out his hand to Jerry. "Thanks again." Then he followed Nathan through the archway. To his surprise, Nathan stopped short of entering the kitchen.

"No one wants you—I thought you might need a breather."

Shaun expelled a breath. "Thanks. I got a little overwhelmed just now." He struggled to regain his composure. "I'm okay." He glanced toward the living room. "Have you met all my friends?"

"Oh yeah."

Shaun chuckled. "Some of them are real characters, I know." Then he looked once more toward the living room. "I'm glad everyone came, but—"

"But now you wish they'd all leave?"

He nodded.

"Don't worry," Nathan told him. "These kinda shindigs don't usually go on all that long." He smiled. "Your dad would be proud of you."

It was the best thing he could have said.

The guests had all gone, and Nathan was clearing up in the kitchen. When he realized how silent the house had become, he went in search of Shaun, and found him sitting on the couch, a photo album open in his lap. He glanced up when Nathan entered.

"Most of these are from before I was born, or when I was little." Shaun shook his head. "Can't remember the last time I took a photo."

Nathan sat beside him. "Remember what Peter

said in his letter. It's time for you to start living again. But just because the funeral is over, that doesn't mean the grief will stop. Your friends will still check in on you. So will I."

Shaun smiled. "I don't know how I would've gotten through all this without you. To be honest, I was dreading today, and not because of the funeral."

"What do you mean?"

"You've been a part of my life for more than six months. And next week, you go back to work, to take care of new patients. It feels strange to think you won't be coming here anymore."

Nathan squeezed Shaun's knee. "We've had this conversation, remember? You're not getting rid of me that easily. I'm gonna keep popping up like a bad penny."

Shaun covered Nathan's hand with his own. "I'm glad to hear that." He gazed at the windows through which could be seen many twinkling colored lights. "Everyone is gearing up for Christmas."

Nathan's plans were set in stone—Momma expected him, and he liked his balls just the way they were—but it pained him that he hadn't given a thought to Shaun over the holidays. "What will you do?"

"I can't even think about a tree. Christmases haven't been the same since Mom died." He swallowed hard. "I mean, I put up the tree for Dad, but... I just can't."

"It's okay not to be in a Christmas mood... *this* year," Nathan told him. "I think you get a pass."

"You're right about grief, you know. It still hurts." Shaun's eyes glistened. "I knew this was coming, right? Once he had that diagnosis, it was a foregone conclusion. So why does it hurt so much?"

Nathan put his arms around Shaun and tugged him close. Shaun didn't put up any resistance, but sobbed quietly into Nathan's shirt. "Okay, so it was a foregone conclusion. Doesn't make it any less of a shock when it finally happens." Shaun clung to him, and he let him.

But I want to do so much more than just hold him. The urge to press his lips to Shaun's, to kiss away his tears and heartache, almost overwhelmed him, and Nathan had to fight to keep his emotions in check. Ben's words rang in his head.

He can't be right—can he?

Chapter Fifteen

December 18

Nathan had barely gotten through the front door before his phone rang. He shook his head when he saw Momma's face. "When you were staying here, did you hide cameras around the place? I literally just got home. Haven't even shaken the snow off my boots or fed Cat yet." The tabby was already circling his ankles, but Nathan knew Cat was all about the food.

"Put me on speaker, then feed the damn cat."

He removed his footwear and coat, then went into the kitchen, Cat trotting after him. Nathan hit the speaker. "What can I do for you, Momma? I'll be seeing you in less than five days." He got the cat food out and began forking it into Cat's bowl. The furball wasted no time diving in, and Nathan filled his blue bowl with fresh water.

"I'm checking up on Shaun. How's he doing?"

"He's okay. A little quieter, maybe."

"You keeping an eye on him?"

Nathan smiled. "I go there every day, even if it's just for a cup of coffee. When he's not at work, he's sorting through his dad's stuff, deciding what to keep, what goes in the trash and what goes to Goodwill."

"That's a tough job. Don't let him do that on his own. Invite yourself over for a pizza or something, and help him out." She sighed. "The memories will swamp him. He'll need a friend."

As if Nathan needed an excuse to visit Shaun. He couldn't keep away. Thankfully, Shaun seemed happy to find him turning up on his doorstep, but Nathan knew that situation wouldn't last. *He'll want his life to get back to normal at some point, and that life won't include me.*

"And still on the subject of Shaun… what's he doing for Christmas?"

Nathan knew Christmas was the last thing on Shaun's mind. "We haven't discussed it." Shaun hadn't brought it up since their talk the day of the funeral.

"What's to discuss? Bring him here with you."

"Excuse me?" Lord, that was just like her, impulsive and generous.

"You heard me."

"And what if he does have plans?"

Momma huffed. "If he had those, he'd have said something. No way am I gonna let that boy sit in that empty house over Christmas, not when there's room here for him."

"Momma, you're gonna have a houseful."

"So what? A skinny thing like Shaun? He won't take up too much space. No, you bring him with you. I'm not gonna take no for an answer. And now that I've got that out of the way…"

Nathan couldn't help smiling. Momma didn't *do* objections—she just rolled right over them.

"You got a new patient?"

"Not exactly. I'm part of a team, working with two or three different patients."

"And it's going okay?"

"It is now," he said with a sigh. "I had to change teams the second day."

"Baby? What's wrong?

"My first patient was an old guy. He took one look at me, and let out a mouthful that I'm not gonna repeat. So… they assigned me to another team. No similar issues so far."

She huffed. "Do I need to guess what he said?

"Nope."

"It happens. I'd *like* to say it's happening less, but I can't. Ignore 'em. If all they see is the color of your skin, or the fact you have different equipment, and they're not willing to look deeper, then don't waste your breath or your energy on 'em."

Different equipment… His momma was awesome.

"Now, you tell Shaun he'll be welcome here."

"Momma…" He loved her for thinking of it, but Shaun was in no mood to celebrate anything right then. Not that Nathan liked the idea of him alone in that house either.

"When your granddaddy passed, I just wanted to… shut down. Your daddy wouldn't let me. I'll make certain no one asks him questions about his dad. All I want is to give him an escape—if he wants it. Give him something completely different to focus on."

"If you're sure there'll be room…"

"I'll *make* room. Now let's change the subject." She paused. "I made a big mistake."

"What do you mean?"

"Jadyn asked if he could decorate the house for the holidays."

Nathan laughed. "Oh God, you didn't."

"I took pity on him, all right? Della was keeping his Christmas… enthusiasm on a tight leash, so I told him he could do what he wanted. Dear *Lord*, the place looks like an explosion in a Christmas factory."

"I can't wait to see it."

"See it? You'll be able to *see* it a mile away."

He chuckled. "I'll call Shaun and tell him your idea."

"Just you remember what I said. That boy needs company." Another pause. "Okay, I gotta go. I have something in the oven."

"Momma… I'll be bringing Cat too." Nathan didn't want to leave him with his neighbor like he usually did. Besides, the kids would love him.

Momma groaned. "Cats and Christmas trees are *not* a good mix." She rolled out a heavy sigh. "Bring him. He's a sweet kitty. He can't cause *that* much damage, right?"

Nathan hoped not.

December 19

Shaun turned the lamps on in the living room. Outside, more snow had fallen, and he'd had to clear a path from the sidewalk to the door. A white carpet lay about twelve inches thick over his front yard.

He wasn't thinking about snow. Nathan had called, and he was stopping by for dinner. It was more than the chance to hear someone else's voice other than his own, however. Nathan's visits brought him a quiet joy that he couldn't fully explain. They also brought him tension, but that was all too understandable. Much as he enjoyed Nathan's company, their conversations, and the moments of laughter dotted here and there, Shaun had to admit they were a strain. He didn't want to fight his attraction to the gentle giant—he yearned to give into it—but he was enough of a realist to know nothing could come of it. Why would it? Sure, Nathan paid him regular visits, but Shaun knew what that was all about. Nathan was checking in on him, out of a sense of duty, and his visits had to have an expiration date eventually.

His phone buzzed, and one glance at the screen made him smile.

I have pizza! Be there in five minutes.

That was something else Shaun liked about Nathan—his timing was awesome. Only that afternoon, Shaun had had a hankering for pizza. Then he caught sight of the brown boxes lined up under the window, and his heart sank. Yet more of Dad on its way to someplace new. He'd kept a few things: Dad's tool chest from when he was younger; his record player and his music collection; and his watch. Shaun could still remember cuddling up to his dad when he was little, listening to its comforting tick.

The doorbell rang, and Shaun hurried to let Nathan in. The odor of sauce and cheese assaulted his nostrils instantly, and his stomach grumbled. "That smells amazing."

"Can we be slobs and eat by the fire? I need to warm up." Nathan handed him the pizza box before taking his boots and coat off.

Shaun laughed. "Sure. We can sit on the rug. Just don't get tomatoes on it. What do you want to drink with it?"

Nathan grinned. "What else? Soda."

Once he'd grabbed a couple of cans from the

kitchen, they sat cross-legged on the rug, the open box between them. That first mouthful was delicious, and Shaun groaned. "Damn, that's good."

Nathan glanced over Shaun's shoulder. "You've gotten more boxes filled, I see."

"Yeah. Almost there."

"How was work?"

Shaun rolled his eyes. "Tiring. And I only worked four hours." Jean had insisted on him starting back part-time. He'd protested that he could work the full six hours, but by the time two-thirty had come around, he'd had enough.

Who knew grief could wipe you out?

Except it was more than grief. It was the day itself.

Shaun paused between bites. "Know what today is?"

Nathan shook his head, but then he widened his eyes. "Yeah, I do. It's Peter's birthday."

He nodded. "I bought a card and a present, right after Thanksgiving. I was walking from my car to the restaurant, and I spotted something in a store window. It was perfect for him." He smiled. "A Christmas sweater." There was a lump in his throat. "It was the kind of thing Mom would've bought for him."

Nathan sighed. "You know this is gonna keep happening for a while, don't you? The first birthday. The first Christmas. New Year's. Easter. Thanksgiving. Wedding anniversary. All those milestones, all those memories…"

"You were right about one thing," Shaun acknowledged.

"Only one? I'll have to do better," Nathan said with a smile.

"When you said he'll never be truly gone, because he's in my heart." He pointed to the mantelpiece, where Dad's letter sat. "I must've read it twenty times already."

"Have you given any thought to his suggestion? You know, about making a change. Unless working in the hospitality industry is your idea of a dream career."

Shaun bit his lip. "I wouldn't go that far. I mean, they're good people to work for, and they've been awesome these past years, but…"

"But you hadn't planned on staying forever."

"No, I hadn't."

"Any idea what you'd like to do if you had the chance?"

Shaun took a bite of pizza before answering. "That letter did get me thinking, but what I came up with was more what I *didn't* wanna do, rather than what I did."

"Such as?"

"I'm not crazy with the idea of a desk job. I like being active."

"Okay, that's a start."

Shaun finished his slice in three bites. "A practical job, one where I get to use my hands… I kinda like that idea."

Nathan picked up another slice. "Electrician."

He snorted. "Hell no. I'd end up electrocuting myself."

"Plumber?"

Shaun wrinkled his nose. "And end up knee-deep in someone's shit? No way."

Nathan cackled. "Tell it like it is, Shaun." He licked his fingers. "Damn, this is good."

Shaun grimaced. "Can you *not* say that right

after I talked about shit? Just... Ew." That earned him another cackle. "I did have one idea, but..." He'd dismissed it as fanciful.

Nathan's eyes sparkled. "Tell me."

"You'll laugh."

"Try me."

"I was looking at Dad's tool chest the other day. Chisels, saws, stuff like that... And it got me thinking. Maybe I could try my hand at carpentry, or cabinet-making. Working with wood at any rate."

Nathan cocked his head to one side. "Wait a minute. *You* were the one who told me you hit your thumb helping your dad build bookcases."

"I was six!" They both laughed.

"If you knew someone in that line, they might be able to advise you, give you an idea of what you'd be letting yourself in for, the kind of training you'd need..."

Shaun smiled. "But I do. Finn."

"Really? That's great. All you gotta do is invite him over for a coffee and a chat."

"Maybe after Christmas." It felt too soon after losing Dad to be changing the direction of his life. *Let me get through next week first.*

"Speaking of Christmas, there's something I want to talk to you about." Nathan took a mouthful of soda. "Momma called. She said I was to bring you with me next week, to spend Christmas with us."

Shaun hastily swallowed his pizza. "I couldn't do that."

"Why not? You know you'll be well-fed—you saw that at Thanksgiving—and you've already met Momma."

"I wouldn't want to be a burden."

"Did it sound like an invitation? It was more like a summons." Nathan leaned back on his hands. "Unless you've got other plans? Maybe you're staying with one of your friends?"

Shaun smiled. "We meet up at New Year's, but Christmas? That's a time for family. And things have changed for a lot of them on that score. Seb's mom comes across as a nightmare, but this year, he'll be with Marcus and *his* family. Sounds like they've adopted Seb. Ben will be with Wade, and Wade's mom and granddad. Finn has Joel and his kids. Dylan and Mark? All they need is each other." His stomach clenched and his throat tightened.

"Hey, what is it?" Nathan leaned forward.

What shocked him was that Nathan had picked up on Shaun's change of mood. "It took me until now to realize something. I'm a little envious of them."

"Why? Because they have someone in their lives?" Shaun nodded. "You haven't had time for a relationship, but that can change now too." Nathan smiled. "I'm not suggesting you have to run off right this second and start dating, but at least you can be open to the possibility."

"Oh, I'm open to it." *With you.* Shaun shoved the thought from his mind. What use was there in torturing himself?

"Now, about Momma's invitation..." Nathan locked gazes with him. "Please, don't make me have to tell her you're alone for Christmas. Have pity on my balls."

Laughter bubbled up out of him before he could stop it. "I didn't realize how much was hanging on my decision. When you put it like that..." Not that he disliked the idea of spending a few days with

Nathan, far from it. "She lives in Augusta, I think you said?"

Nathan nodded. "I'm going there Wednesday, and I'll be back Sunday. Cat is going too. So… do I tell her you're coming?"

Shaun sighed. "With the fate of your balls hanging in the balance? How could I say no?" Besides, when was the last time he'd enjoyed a real family Christmas?

Dad wouldn't want me to be on my own. Neither would Mom.

Spending almost five days in the company of Cassie and her family didn't sound as if it would be a hardship. On the contrary… Five days in the company of his own gentle giant with the strong hands and stronger arms, and eyes that saw so much, promised to be exactly what Shaun needed.

Chapter Sixteen

December 23

"Was your boss okay with you taking time off?" Nathan asked as he drove across Memorial Bridge, its dark surface devoid of snow, piles of white flanking it. On either side of the Kennebec river, colored lights twinkled against the evening sky.

"Yeah. Jean—she's Sandy's wife. Sandy's the cook—told me she was happy I wouldn't be on my own." Shaun paused. "I'm sorry you couldn't leave any earlier, but they were stuck for servers today, so I said I'd work till five."

Nathan smiled. "Don't worry about it. As long as we're there in time for dinner, Momma won't mind." He'd called to give her an ETA. He took a right onto Stone Street, then another right onto East Chestnut Street. "We're almost there. Is Cat still asleep?"

Shaun twisted to look at the back seat where the pet carrier sat. "Yeah."

"Wait till he sees Momma's tree. We're gonna have to keep an eye on him. And make sure Joey doesn't pull his tail or his ears."

When they finally turned into Brooks Street, Shaun caught his breath. "Wow. Would you look at that house? I reckon they could see it from space, it has so many lights."

Dear Lord...

Nathan coughed. "That's Momma's house. And

before you say another word, this is all my brother
Jadyn's doing." He parked the car behind the red
Honda in the driveway, and they got out. "I think my
balls are safe this year. Jadyn's? That's another matter."

"It's a cute house."

Nathan stared at the steep sloping roof, its gable
dripping with blue icicle lights that spread along the
gutters. He'd always liked the cream cedar shakes and
red trim, and the front porch with its swing and
reddish-brown wooden railing. Every window was
covered in a net of tiny white lights, and a decorated
tree stood in the front bay window. The normal
expanse of green between the house and the sidewalk
was covered in snow, but every inch of space was taken
up with moving reindeer, Santas, and elves, all lit up.
From a speaker under the porch came the sound of
cheesy Christmas music. Colored lights wound around
the trunk of the huge tree standing in the yard.

He shook his head. "Next time Jadyn asks if he
can decorate, Momma won't be so quick to say yes."

"Unca!"

Nathan grinned at the little boy standing in the
doorway, Jadyn behind him. "Joey!"

"I'll get the bags and Cat, you go say hi to your
nephew," Shaun told him, taking the keys from his
hand.

"Thanks." Nathan hurried up the cleared path
to the wooden steps that led to the front door. He
swung Joey up into his arms. "You're getting big."

Jadyn chuckled. "And more of a handful every
day." He glanced over Nathan's shoulder. "So that's
Shaun, huh?"

Nathan narrowed his gaze. "What does *that*
mean?"

"Oh, nothing. Momma's been talking about him." Jadyn held up his hands. "Don't panic, we know the score. We'll handle him with kid gloves."

"There's no need for that. He won't break. Just don't talk about his dad, that's all." He clammed up at the sound of Shaun's footsteps behind him.

Jadyn gave Shaun a wide smile. "Welcome to the madhouse. I'm Nathan's brother, Jadyn. Come on in. Momma's got a fire going." He regarded Nathan with twinkling eyes. "Just a heads up—she made eggnog."

"Oh dear Lord." Nathan lowered Joey to the ground, then stood aside to let Shaun enter.

Joey's eyes widened when he spied the pet carrier. "Kitty!"

Jadyn groaned. "Great. Now he'll want a kitty."

"Are you or Della allergic?" Nathan asked. When Jadyn shook his head, Nathan grinned. "Then be a good dad and get him a kitty."

Shaun put the bags down at the foot of the stairs, gazing at his surroundings.

"Unca! Lights!" Joey pointed to the front yard.

Nathan chuckled as he closed the door behind them. "I bet Della loves this."

"Hold onto your ass. She does."

He blinked. "How come? Was she visited by three ghosts?"

Jadyn snorted. "Hell no. She's just happy none of this stuff is at our place. You know what? She said I could only put up one Christmas tree this year."

Nathan gave a gasp of mock horror. "However are you coping?"

"If you don't get your butt in this kitchen right now and give me a hug, there will be no biscuits and gravy for you in the morning," Momma hollered.

Shaun snickered. "Well, don't just stand there."

"And I was addressing both of you," she added.

Nathan beckoned him to follow, and headed for the kitchen. Momma stood at the stove, stirring something in a pan. "Supper is almost ready." She turned down the heat, then wiped her hands before holding her arms in invitation.

Nathan hugged her. "Hey, Momma."

She kissed his cheek before releasing him. "'Bout time." Then she beamed at Shaun. "Hey, sweetheart. Got a hug for me?" Without waiting for a response, Momma enfolded him in her arms. "Glad you could join us."

Shaun chuckled. "Did I have a choice?"

"No." She let him go. "I made eggnog this afternoon. Want some?"

Nathan stood behind her, mouthing *No. No.*

"I'd love some," Shaun told her. "Mom used to make it, but I was only allowed a small glass."

Nathan rolled his eyes. *Can't say I didn't warn him.* Momma's eggnog was lethal. Phoebe used to joke it could strip paint with its fumes alone.

Jadyn snorted from the doorway. "Trust me," he muttered. "A small glass is plenty."

Momma jerked her head in his direction. "I heard that." She patted Shaun's cheek. "Let me show you where you'll be sleeping." She peered at Nathan. "You come too." She led them out of the kitchen, stopping while they picked up their bags, then headed upstairs. "Your sister and Leo are out doing some last-minute Christmas shopping, and taking Kelsey to see Santa." When she reached the top, she opened the first door on the left. "I've put you in here."

"Who—me or Shaun?"

Momma turned slowly to meet his gaze. "Both of you." She gestured for them to enter. "There's a foldaway cot under the window, and clean bed linen on the chair."

Shaun glanced at Nathan. "Is there a problem?"

It wasn't as if he could tell the truth. *No, everything's fine. I just didn't want to be sharing a room with you, because that would feel too much like torture, having you so close.*

Momma was looking at him as if she knew exactly what was going on inside his head. "I've got a houseful. Where did you *think* I was gonna put him—in the shed?" She pointed to the comforter. "And don't let that damn cat sleep on there. He'll shed fur all over it."

Nathan snorted. "Cat will sleep wherever he pleases."

"Momma, should this smell like it's burning?" Jadyn yelled from below.

"My gravy!" She pushed past Nathan and made a dash for the stairs.

"No running, Momma!" he called after her. "Not unless you *want* to end up in the Emergency Room for Christmas." Nathan shook his head.

Shaun put his bag on the bed. "Well… this is… cozy."

Nathan sat on the edge of the mattress. "I'll take the foldaway cot."

"You're kidding, right?" Shaun cackled. "Of course, watching you trying to fit all of your six feet whatever inches into it will be entertaining." His eyes gleamed. "*I'll* take it."

Nathan was forced to agree he had a point. "You okay sharing a room?" He hadn't given it a moment's thought. Momma had said she'd have space for Shaun.

Momma…

Nathan had an inkling he'd just been set up.

"Sure. It's fine." Shaun's nonchalance eased his disquiet.

It's just me that's making a big deal outta this. It was also a reminder that whatever Nathan's feelings were for Shaun, they weren't reciprocated.

It was the kind of reminder that made his heart sink.

"Supper in five minutes," Momma shouted.

He'd deal with her later, not that he expected her to tell the truth.

Shaun had the feeling he'd been adopted. Everyone had been so welcoming, from Jadyn and his wife Della, to Phoebe and her partner Leo. Phoebe's little boy, Kelsey, was four years old, and the way he looked out for his little cousin was adorable. Joey and Kelsey hadn't joined the adults for supper, but were seated at the sweetest little table, and Joey was babbling in a nonsensical way that probably only made sense to Kelsey. Jadyn had said he could string three words together to make a sentence, and watching Joey laugh and giggle warmed Shaun's heart.

Cassie caught him staring at them, and he smiled. "They're cute kids. And that table is awesome."

"My husband made that for Nathan when he

was Joey's age. Then it was Phoebe's, and then Jadyn's."

"And next year it'll be Angel's too," Jadyn murmured.

"Where kitty?" Joey called out.

"Kitty is in the kitchen, asleep," Jadyn told him. "You can see him when you've finished your supper."

Cassie chuckled. "He's curled up by the warm air vent."

"There's more mashed potato if you want some." Nathan pointed to the serving dish. "Grab it while you can."

Shaun didn't need a second invitation. He helped himself to another spoonful, then reached for the gravy jug. "This gravy is delicious." It had *all* been delicious: meatloaf, green beans, potatoes...

"Cassie's gravy is a food group all on its own," Leo said with a smile. Shaun had liked the quiet, studious man from the start. Nathan had said Leo taught science at the local high school, and that he and Phoebe had been childhood sweethearts.

Leo regarded Shaun with interest. "So, what do you do, Shaun?"

"I work in a restaurant in Portland. Well, I do for the moment." He smiled. "I'm looking to maybe change things up a bit."

Cassie widened her eyes. "Oh? You given any thought to what you might do?"

"Nothing concrete." He gave a shrug. "I did think about going back to school. Maybe a trade school. I'll look into it after Christmas. I thought I might enjoy working with my hands."

Cassie beamed. "You and my husband would've gotten along just fine."

Della wiped her lips with her napkin. After hearing Jadyn, Shaun had expected her to be the female equivalent of Scrooge, but that wasn't the case. She'd greeted Shaun warmly, and watching her with Joey and Angel revealed how much she adored her children. *Maybe she's not as much into Christmas as Jadyn.* That raised an internal smile. *No one* could be as much into it as Jadyn. Their kids needed a little balance, after all.

Della met Shaun's gaze. "Are you ready to do battle in the morning?"

"Excuse me?"

"As soon as breakfast is over, Joey and Kelsey will want to go out and play in the snow."

"Kelsey's dying to build a snowman," Phoebe added. "And you *will* get roped into either that or a snowball fight, so don't even think about making other plans."

Shaun smiled. "I can't remember the last time I did either of those things."

"And *where* are they gonna build a snowman?" Nathan jerked his head toward the front of the house. "It's kinda covered out there."

Della bit her lip. "You noticed that, huh?"

Yeah, Shaun liked her.

"The back yard is a Christmas-free zone," Cassie declared. "Snow's probably that deep out there, it'll bury Joey."

Nathan's gaze met Shaun's. "You up for building a snowman?"

If it meant spending time with Nathan, Shaun was certainly up for it. "You bet."

Whatever reluctance he'd expressed at the thought of burdening Cassie had dissipated. With no fanfare, no fuss, the whole family had pulled him into their celebrations, and made him feel part of the proceedings.

Maybe that's the magic of Christmas.

After the heartache of the past few weeks, Shaun could do with a little magic.

The kids were in bed, and the adults sat around the fire, drinking alcohol in some guise or other. Shaun was on the couch next to Nathan, holding a glass of eggnog and staring into the flickering flames. Cat had been let out of the kitchen and was stretched out at the foot of the Christmas tree, gazing up at it.

Jadyn was watching him. "You wait and see. He'll wait till no one's looking, and then he'll attack."

"If he does, it'll be a first," Nathan commented. He leaned into Shaun and gestured to the glass in Shaun's hand. "You don't have to finish it," he whispered.

Shaun chuckled. Cassie was in the kitchen. "I like it," he insisted.

Nathan blinked. "You're not just being polite, are you? You really do like it."

"Hey, *someone* had to, eventually, right?" Jadyn's grin seemed to be a permanent feature.

"It tastes like my mom's," Shaun told them, just as Cassie came back into the room, carrying a plate of cookies. He laughed as Nathan lurched up off the couch and made a beeline for them.

Cassie winked at him. "What did I say about a New York minute?"

"Thank God you're here," Jadyn said to Nathan after taking a sip of whiskey. When Nathan gave him a quizzical glance, Jadyn inclined his head toward Cassie. "Maybe she'll ask *you* to step in when she needs a longer arm, and we won't be facing trips to the ER."

Cassie's eyes narrowed. "Now, don't exaggerate. I just slipped, okay? And I didn't break or sprain anything."

"What did she do this time?" Nathan asked.

"'*She*'? I'm right here, aren't I?"

"Sure, but Jadyn will tell me the truth."

Jadyn pointed to the ceiling. "She got up on a chair to fix that."

Shaun raised his gaze, and spotted a sprig of plastic mistletoe hanging above the rug in front of the fire.

"Since when do you put up mistletoe?" Nathan demanded. "And Jadyn's right. You could've fallen."

"But I didn't, did I? Stop your whining." Cassie rolled her eyes. "You'll notice the tree is missing something. I saved that job for you." She grabbed a cardboard box from under its boughs. "Here you go."

Nathan removed the lid, and Shaun had to smile at the sight of an angel in flowing bronze and gold robes, its wings looking a little battered. "How old is that?"

Cassie chuckled. "So old, I'm not gonna embarrass myself by revealing it."

Nathan stretched up and sat the angel on top of the tree. "There. Where it belongs." The others fell silent, and it felt like a special moment.

Cassie caught Shaun's gaze. "My husband

bought that angel, our first Christmas after we were married."

"Wow. *That* old," Leo said in a stage whisper. Phoebe giggled.

Shaun cleared his throat. "So what's the drill around here? Are you a presents-on-Christmas-Eve kinda family, or do you wait until Christmas morning?" Mom had always insisted he wait until morning, a tradition that had gone by the wayside in recent years.

"The adults get to open presents after midnight on Christmas Eve," Nathan told him. "Christmas morning is strictly for the kids."

"Remember how you said you were gonna write a letter to Santa one year?" Phoebe chuckled. "You were going to complain because there were no presents under the tree for Momma and Daddy."

"How was I to know they'd opened them all the night before?" Nathan remonstrated. "I was seven, for God's sake. And *you* only remember 'cause Momma kept telling that story. You were four."

"Aw, that's so cute." Shaun couldn't help smiling at the image in his head: a little Nathan, incensed by Santa's apparent neglect.

"You wanna see cute?" Cassie reached into a bookcase next to her armchair, and removed a hefty photo album.

"Momma. No." Nathan glared at her. "Shaun does *not* want to see those."

"Hey, I can speak for myself, you know." He covered his mouth with his hand, unable to suppress his yawn.

"Maybe tomorrow," Cassie suggested. "You need some sleep. You've got a heavy day tomorrow." Her eyes gleamed. "And you will *all* keep out of my kitchen, you got that? I don't need help. Especially *your* kinda help," she added, pointing at Jadyn and Nathan.

Della laughed. "What Cassie means is, they like to test the cooking. Whether she wants them to or not."

"It's a heavy responsibility, but someone's gotta do it, right?" Jadyn winked at Nathan. "I think it's pretty selfless of us to be willing to step up to the plate every year."

Shaun was still laughing about it as they climbed the stairs after saying goodnight to everyone. "I like your family," he said as they reached their room.

"They like you too." Nathan closed the door. "Glad you came?"

He smiled. "Yeah. Thank your momma for insisting. This was just what I needed." He inclined his head toward the door. "Will Cat be okay downstairs?"

"He's got his basket, his favorite blanket... And of course the most important item."

"What's that?"

Nathan grinned. "His litterbox. Cat'll be fine."

Shaun unfolded the cot, and quickly made it up, then reached into his bag for his toothbrush and toothpaste. "Where do I…"

"The bathroom's next door," Nathan told him as he pulled his sweater up and over his head.

Shaun hurried out of the room, grateful for the opportunity not to watch Nathan undressing. *Oh God. I hope he wears pajamas.* Shaun wasn't sure he could cope with seeing Nathan naked, or as near as damn it. Then he remembered he'd be sleeping in his briefs. *Maybe I should've thought about that.*

By the time he got back to the bedroom, Nathan was in bed, lying on his back, his arms folded beneath his head. Shaun tried not to stare at the expanse of smooth, firm chest and toned, muscular arms. The sheet covered him from the waist down, and the comforter hid the rest, for which Shaun was thankful. But that first glimpse of Nathan's bare torso told him Nathan's body was as handsome as his face.

With his back to the bed, Shaun stripped down to his briefs, and climbed into the cot. He covered himself with the sheets, doing his best not to glance in Nathan's direction.

"You comfy?"

Shaun couldn't ignore that. He rolled onto his side to face Nathan, and found him in a similar position, his head propped up by his hand. "I was right." When Nathan gave him an inquiring glance, Shaun smiled. "You couldn't have slept in here." He sighed. "Thank you."

"For what?"

"Not taking no for an answer, for one thing. And for making this so... easy."

Nathan frowned. "What do you mean?"

"Your brother, your sister...No one's asked any personal questions." He'd expected the third degree but when it hadn't materialized, profound relief had swept through him.

"That was Momma's doing."

Shaun could believe that. "Your momma is amazing. Come to think of it, your whole family is pretty special. And your nephews are precious."

Nathan's smile reached his eyes. "Still wanna have two or three kids?"

He laughed. "Yeah. Being around all of you... It makes me wish I'd had brothers and sisters. I envy you."

"You seem to be doing a lot of that lately."

"Huh?"

"Envying. You said something about envying your friends too. You know, the ones who've gotten themselves boyfriends. Like I said, maybe it's your turn now."

Shaun shifted onto his back and stared at the ceiling. "I'm not in any hurry. Mom and Dad didn't find each other till they were in their late twenties. Dad was almost thirty. I figure there's hope for me yet."

"Do you really wanna wait till you're thirty?"

He chuckled. "No, not really. But I'm not looking. I'm a huge believer in fate. It'll happen when it's right." He turned his head to look at Nathan. "What about you?"

Nathan's eyes gleamed. "Momma wants me to settle down. But I believe in fate too. Who knows? The perfect guy could be right under my nose."

God, how Shaun yearned for that to be true. *Maybe fate brought us together. Maybe we're* supposed *to be together.*

The only thing stopping him from revealing what lay in his heart was the fact that until a short two weeks ago, Nathan had been in his house in a professional capacity, and Shaun had been the guy who'd hired him.

He wouldn't want me. There had to be all manner of reasons why Nathan would want someone who was Shaun's polar opposite.

He just didn't want to think what those reasons might be.

The room was plunged into darkness. "Get some sleep," Nathan murmured.

Only if I can dream of you.

Sleep didn't come right away. Shaun lay there,

reflecting on his day. He hadn't lied when he'd told Nathan how much he appreciated the welcome everyone had given him, but their warmth and generosity hadn't been able to completely banish the ache inside. *Dad would've loved this.* He hadn't been far from Shaun's thoughts all evening, and when a wave of melancholy crashed over him, he'd done his best to paste on a smile. He didn't want to invite comment or sympathy.

"It's exhausting, isn't it?" Nathan's voice came out of the darkness, low and deep.

"What is?"

"Wearing a mask all the time. Being sociable, when your heart's not in it."

Shaun was about to ask how Nathan had known, when he realized Nathan spoke from experience. "There were times tonight when I felt guilty."

"Because you were having a good time, when you were supposed to be grieving?" Nathan sighed. "I get that. It's not as if you've forgotten Peter. You just... put aside the hurt for a few hours. He'd want that for you. So listen. Anytime over the next few days, if you need to come up here and be alone for a while, you do that. No one will say a word. Okay?"

Shaun breathed a little easier. "Okay. And thank you."

"One more thing. If you need a hug, you only have to ask."

Warmth trickled through him. "I'll hold you to that." He closed his eyes and let sleep take him.

Chapter Seventeen

December 24

Nathan opened his eyes before his alarm went off on his phone. Several times during the night, he'd woken and lay there in the dark, listening to Shaun's breathing. *At least he got some sleep.* From downstairs filtered the familiar sounds of Momma at work in the kitchen.

Then he remembered. *I want a word with Momma.*

Nathan got out of bed as quietly as he could. Shaun could sleep a little longer. He pulled on his jeans, sweater, and a pair of thick socks, then crept out of the room.

Momma was standing at the sink, humming to herself. She turned her head as he entered, and grinned. "You smelled the coffee, didn't you?"

Coffee could wait.

"It's no accident, is it, that I ended up sharing a room with Shaun?"

"To quote you... I don't know what you're talking about." She wiped her hands.

"Momma…"

She folded her arms. "You still in denial? Child, you have feelings for that boy, and don't you be lying to me and sayin' you don't." Her eyes twinkled. "But it's okay… Momma's got your back."

"Momma…"

She gave him an innocent stare. "You just

needed a little push, that's all."

He glared at her. "No. No pushing." The door opened, and Shaun came into the room. Nathan aimed one more hard stare at Momma, then pointed to the coffee pot. "Morning. Help yourself. I'll have a cup too."

Shaun scraped his fingers through his black hair. "Morning."

"You sleep okay?" Momma asked.

He nodded. "That foldaway cot was really comfortable."

Momma glared at Nathan. "You made him sleep in the cot?"

"He insisted!" Nathan protested. "And besides, if *I'd* slept in it, my legs would've stuck out over the edge."

She narrowed her gaze. "Hmm." Then she smiled at Shaun. "Morning, honey. Breakfast won't be long. We've got biscuits, sausage gravy, hash browns, eggs… That'll set you up for the day."

Nathan poured two cups of coffee, and handed one to Shaun. "Don't expect much conversation yet, Momma. Shaun needs more caffeine to get his brain into gear."

Shaun chuckled. "You know me so well."

Yeah—and I want to know you better.

Nathan stood by the back door, watching Jadyn, Della, Shaun, Joey and Kelsey as they piled a heap of snow in the center of the yard. Momma had given them a couple of potatoes for eyes, a carrot for its nose, and small assorted buttons to form its mouth.

"It needs a scarf and a hat," Nathan murmured.

Phoebe joined him, handing him a cup of coffee. "Maybe there's an old one of Daddy's Momma wouldn't mind giving them."

Nathan turned to stare at her. "And how come you're not out there, helping?"

She glared at him. "I could ask you the same question. And *I've* got an excuse. I got my nails done yesterday, that's why." They both chuckled.

"For your information, I've already done a stint outside. I came in to warm up." He didn't think it would be long before Shaun joined him. He kept casting glances toward the window where Nathan stood.

She sipped her coffee, her gaze fixed on the snowman-building crew. "So... Shaun..."

"What about him?" Nathan had expected comments before this from one of his siblings, but he'd put his money on Jadyn.

"I like him." She glanced at him, her eyes sparkling. "In case that's important to you."

"Why would it be important?" She was fishing. She had nothing to go on.

He hoped.

"In case we're going to be seeing more of him in the future." Another sideways glance. "We *are* going to be seeing him again—aren't we?"

Damn her.

Phoebe sighed. "Nathan... he's a nice guy. He's

smart, kind, thoughtful… Momma thinks highly of him, and that's as good an endorsement as you're gonna get. So all I want to know is… How do you feel about him?"

Nathan kept his gaze locked on the snowy scene outside. "Doesn't matter what I feel, not if this is a one-way street." It was no surprise she knew he was gay. He didn't figure Jadyn and Momma would've kept quiet about that.

"And is it?"

Nathan jerked his head to stare at her. "What does that mean?"

"It *means* I watched him at supper last night. The way he looked at you whenever you spoke. I just have the feeling there's something there." She smiled. "Plus, I think he's perfect for you."

Nathan snorted. "That wasn't what Momma said. She asked if I had a death wish, wanting to date a white guy."

"Was that before or after she met him?"

"Before."

Phoebe shook her head. "Sometimes I think Grandmomma knew what she was doing when she named Momma Cassandra. And it doesn't matter that Shaun's white, because it obviously doesn't bother him that you're Black." She gave him a one-armed hug. "I just want my big brother to be happy. It's about damn time."

"Who says I'm unhappy?"

She kissed his cheek. "I *know* you, remember? And I want to dance at your wedding, or your commitment ceremony, or whatever gay guys do, while I can still enjoy it. So don't leave it too long before you tell him how you feel." She grinned. "He might surprise you. It *is* Christmas, after all." She nudged him with her elbow. "Now get out there and help them give that snowman a face. You have no excuse." She wiggled her fingers, the light dancing on the sparkly nail polish.

Nathan laughed and handed her his cup. "Yes, ma'am."

He still had time to stuff snow down the back of Shaun's neck, after all.

Shaun had a warm, purring cushion in his lap. "Cat likes me." He stroked Cat's silken fur.

"I hate to disillusion you," Nathan said with a chuckle beside him, "but if you've got a pulse, fingers to scratch with, or warmth to steal, Cat'll love you."

It was almost midnight. The kids went to sleep hours before, and Shaun had spent most of the day with them. Once the snowman had been built, the snowballs had started flying, and Shaun had discovered that Nathan was an awesome shot. Of course, once that first trickle of ice had made contact with Shaun's back, he'd had to retaliate, and war was suddenly declared in Cassie's back yard. By the time everyone had come inside for lunch, most of them had needed a change of clothes. Once that was out of the way, Kelsey and Joey had wanted to play with Cat. They'd tied lengths of tinsel to the end of a pole, and had spent hours dangling it, watching Cat leap into the air to grab at the twinkling strands. Then Kelsey had gotten out his toy cars, and he and Joey had spent ages zooming them all over the dining table and the floor.

"Still want kids?" Nathan murmured.

He laughed. "They weren't that exhausting." In fact, it had been a lot of fun. He dug Nathan in the ribs with his elbow. "And you were by far the biggest kid out there."

"I was, wasn't I?" Nathan's preening had him chuckling.

"Okay, time for gifts and eggnog before bed," Cassie announced, carrying in a tray of glasses and a jug. "And it won't harm none of you to just have a sip."

The chorus of mutterings was yet another thing to make Shaun smile.

Under the tree were all the presents that had accumulated once the kids had disappeared. Shaun had snuck a few under there too.

"This is when Nathan gets to play Santa," Jadyn confided. "He's done this every year since we lost Daddy." He grinned. "Except we can't get him to put on a Santa suit."

"That's because they don't make 'em in my size," Nathan declared. He got up from the couch. "Okay. Someone tell me when it gets to midnight."

Shaun grabbed his phone. "You've got thirty seconds. I'll do a countdown." He held up one finger, and the room fell silent. "Ten, nine, eight, seven…"

The others joined in. "Six, five, four, three, two, one…"

Nathan smiled. "Merry Christmas, everyone."

It seemed to be the signal the family had been waiting for. Everybody stood, and hugs were exchanged. Cat leaped from Shaun's lap as Cassie hauled him to his feet. Shaun's throat tightened as he too was hugged. Nathan was the last, and Shaun gave as good as he got.

"Merry Christmas, Nathan."

Warm breath tickled his ear. "Merry Christmas, Shaun."

"Okay, enough hugging," Jadyn protested. "Someone give me a present!"

Nathan rolled his eyes. "You're first on my list, if only to shut you up."

For the next fifteen minutes or so, Nathan handed out the brightly colored gifts, the wrapping paper ending up in a pile in the middle of the floor. Shaun had given chocolate, figuring no one would be unhappy with that, and judging by the smiles, he'd made a good choice. He was surprised to find a couple of gifts had his name on them. The large squishy one was from Cassie.

"Hey, I didn't expect anything."

Cassie waved her hand. "It's just a little something. I didn't want you to feel left out."

It didn't *feel* like a little something.

Shaun tore the paper, and a soft, dark blue sweater slid into his lap. There was no label in the neckline. Then it hit him. "You made this."

She nodded.

He held it up. "It looks as if it's my size too. How did you know?"

Cassie bit back a smile. "I checked out one of your sweaters when I was there for Thanksgiving. I've been knitting it since then. You like it?"

Shaun hugged it against him. "I love it." Cassie beamed, then got on with opening her own presents. It wasn't until a few minutes had passed that her words sank in. *She only met me the once, and yet she took the time to make this?*

Then he realized he still had one gift left to open, but before he could remove the wrapping, Cassie cleared her throat. "Well folks, it's past midnight, and you *know* Joey and Kelsey will be up at the crack of dawn, too excited to sit still. So... everyone with a child in this house? Go to bed and get some sleep. Nathan? You and Shaun make sure the fire is completely out and everywhere is locked up before you come up."

"And are you going to bed too?" Nathan asked her.

Cassie grinned. "I have three children and three grandchildren under my roof. Damn straight I'm going to bed."

"Actually, Momma? You have three and a third grandchildren," Phoebe said with a smile. "We were going to tell you tomorrow, but I couldn't resist, not with an opening like that."

Cassie let out a gasp, and there were *aws* from Della and Jadyn. Nathan was the first to hug her, and the others followed suit. Cassie had tears in her eyes. "That's one hell of a Christmas present." She gave Nathan a meaningful stare, and Shaun didn't need to be a mind reader to know what that look meant.

Your turn.

Once everyone was done congratulating Phoebe and Leo, they piled upstairs after saying goodnight. Nathan went into the kitchen, and Shaun sat on the rug to enjoy the fire before it died. Then he remembered the little gift. The tag said *From Nathan.* He slit the shiny red paper with his fingernail to expose a black box. Shaun lifted the lid to find a bracelet made of woven brown leather strands, joined by two metal clasps.

Nathan returned with two glasses of eggnog.

"Here." He stilled at the sight of the box. "Ah. You opened it."

"It's pretty."

Nathan joined him on the rug, sitting cross-legged. He placed the glasses on the hearth. "Look inside."

Shaun frowned. "Inside?" Then he saw there was engraving on the clasps. He peered closer, and his throat seized. On one side was the name *Peter* and on the other was *Laura*.

"It was an impulse," Nathan confessed.

"It was a beautiful impulse," Shaun said with a croak. He opened the clasps. "Help me put it on?"

Nathan's fingers trembled a little as he fastened the bracelet around Shaun's right wrist. "There. It looks good on you."

"Thank you. So much." He wanted to say more, but the words wouldn't come.

Nathan smiled. "Hey. Here we are again, on the rug. Only, there's no pizza this time."

Shaun was still too overwhelmed by the sweet gift to speak. They both lapsed into silence. Nathan stared into the fire, and Shaun took advantage of the chance to sip a little eggnog to lubricate his throat. He gazed around him at the room illuminated by firelight. Cards stood on every flat surface, and lights dripped from the mantelpiece. The ceiling was the only clear space, except for the small sprig of plastic mistletoe hanging above their heads.

He looked at it with a smile. "Mom used to hang a bunch of mistletoe from the archway." The number of times he'd caught her and dad kissing under it...

Nathan said nothing for a moment. Finally he

expelled a breath. "So… have you ever been kissed under the mistletoe?"

Shaun told himself it was an innocent question, one he felt compelled to answer truthfully. "No, but that's only because… I've never been kissed."

Nathan stared at him with parted lips. "You never met the right girl?"

His heartbeat raced. "Never had the time, the opportunity, or the inclination. Oh, I could've made time, and then I'm sure the opportunity would've presented itself, but…" He met Nathan's gaze. "I never met the right… person."

And then I met you.

Nathan was so still. "Tell me… how would the right person look? Would you know them if you saw them?"

Shaun's heart pounded. *What if this is the only chance I get?*

It was now or never.

His face grew hot. "Well… he's taller than me." He didn't miss Nathan's sharp intake of breath, and knew it to be a reaction to his choice of pronoun. "He has dark brown eyes, a really deep brown. His hair is a mass of black curls that usually needs to be trimmed." His heart thumped. "And if Mom were alive, she'd probably say he gives Denzel Washington a run for his money."

Nathan swallowed hard. "Sounds like a pretty precise description. How long have you had your eye on this guy?"

"A while," he replied honestly. "Only, there was never the right moment."

"And is now the right moment? If someone wanted to be the first to kiss you?"

Shaun gave the mistletoe another glance before looking Nathan in the eye. "Then he'd be in the right place. So... why don't you give it a try?"

Nathan took Shaun's glass from his hand and placed it on the hearth. He unfolded his long legs and knelt up. "Come here." He crooked his fingers.

Oh God.

Shaun knelt in front of him, his pulse rapid as Nathan cupped his cheek, gently stroking his beard, all the while moving closer until he could feel Nathan's breath on his face. He waited for Nathan to zero in on his lips.

Nothing.

Shaun had had it with the slow lane. He brought both hands to Nathan's nape, pulled him in, and pressed his mouth to Nathan's, conscious of warm hands on his back, gentle hands that stroked and caressed.

"Shaun," Nathan whispered against his lips.

Shaun held Nathan's head steady, his heart still beating like ten thousand drums as he took a step out of his comfort zone, exploring Nathan with his tongue.

Nathan pulled back. "Wow. Fast learner."

"Is that a complaint?"

Nathan grinned. "Hell no." Then Shaun's mouth was claimed in a kiss that curled his toes, sent heat surging through him and what felt like every drop of blood in his body making a beeline for his dick.

Noise above their heads froze them.

Nathan glanced up. "That's Momma. She's not in bed yet. But maybe we should be."

Oh dear *God*, the thoughts that hurtled through Shaun's fevered brain... *Stop that.* He sought refuge in practical matters. "I'll put the fire out, you make sure everything's locked up and Cat is in his basket."

"Meet me upstairs?"

A nod was as much as Shaun could manage.

Once they were in the room, Shaun's recent boldness fled him. A kiss? He could handle a kiss. Anything else? Not in Cassie's house. Okay, so he was a virgin. That didn't mean he was in a hurry to change that, not while he was surrounded by Nathan's family.

Nathan closed the door. "Can we go back to what we were doing downstairs?"

Shaun was all for that.

Those strong arms he'd dreamed about held him against Nathan's chest, and he tilted his head back to receive Nathan's kiss. Shaun wrapped his arms around Nathan's waist.

This is a dream, right?

"I've wanted to do this for so long," Nathan whispered. "But I thought you were straight. And then there was the whole I-work-for-you business, and—"

Shaun stopped Nathan's words with his hand. "I'm gay. I've always been gay. This isn't a recent thing, okay?" He sighed. "And I do understand. I'd never had said a word while… while Dad was alive. But… everything's different."

Nathan nodded. "You're free to be yourself. To do what you want." He stilled. "So… where do you want to sleep tonight?"

Shaun shivered. "With you. If that's okay." He smiled. "I know the foldaway cot was more comfortable than I'd expected, but I'd still prefer to sleep in your bed." He bit his lip. "Another first. Never shared a bed before."

Nathan coughed. "That's not exactly true."

"What do you mean?"

Nathan released him and sat on the edge of the bed. "You know that dream you had? About falling off your bike, and your dad holding you all night long?"

Shaun was lost. "Yeah, but—" *Wait a minute.* "That was you, wasn't it?"

Nathan nodded. "You fell asleep in your robe, so I covered you up. I only meant to hold you when you seemed unsettled, but you felt so good."

Without a word but with a pounding heart, Shaun removed his sweater. He tossed it onto the cot bed, then unfastened his waistband, pulled his socks off, and shoved his jeans to his ankles before stepping out of them, leaving his briefs in place. He gazed at Nathan who hadn't moved. "Well?" He affected a nonchalance that was pure bluff. "Are you planning on sleeping in your clothes?"

Nathan rose to his feet and undressed, piling his clothes on top of Shaun's.

Shaun's breath hitched at the sight of Nathan's body, bare before him, his black briefs leaving little to the imagination. He forced himself not to stare, but instead pulled back the comforter and climbed into bed. "This time I wanna remember it."

Nathan climbed in beside him, and Shaun covered them both. Nathan held his arm wide. "Wanna cuddle?"

Shaun smiled. "Thought you'd never ask." He closed the gap between them, snuggling against Nathan's warm body, nuzzling his neck. "If your mom walks in, we're sharing body heat 'cause I was cold, okay?"

Don't think about him being mostly naked. Don't think about the fact that our bodies are touching. Don't think about how amazing this feels.

Nathan chuckled, and it reverberated through his chest. "You really think she's gonna believe that?"

He laughed. "No." Then Nathan's hand was on his face, Nathan's lips claimed his, and Shaun melted into another lingering kiss. This one was less about heat and more about sweetness, and that was just perfect.

"I could do this all night," Shaun whispered.

"Me too," Nathan confessed. "So I think I'll just kiss you until you fall asleep."

Shaun craned his neck to look at Nathan's face. "Is this real?"

"God, I hope so." Nathan's fingers were under Shaun's chin as he kissed him once more. "I've been dreaming of doing this for so long, I'd better wake up and find you're still in my arms."

"I don't plan on going anywhere." He paused. "I know I said what to say if your mom walked in, but I was kidding, all right?"

"Relax," Nathan said with a chuckle. "I locked the door."

Shaun sighed. "Okay." Nathan was warm, his body was firm, and he smelled so damn good.

I could get to like this.

What he didn't want to think about was what happened once he was home, and it was back to reality.

Nathan pressed his lips to Shaun's hair. "Sleep, sweetheart."

"If I sleep, I miss this," he murmured drowsily.

"Then we'll do it all over again when you wake up. Promise."

Shaun thought that sounded pretty goddamn perfect.

Chapter Eighteen

December 25

Nathan opened his eyes. Shaun lay on his side, facing away from him. Nathan took a moment to admire the smooth, creamy expanse of skin, the dip of his spine, his tousled hair against the pillow. He'd fought hard not to stare during Shaun's tantalizing striptease the previous night, and once they'd lain beneath the covers, his hands had ached to touch, caress, stroke…

Sharing a bed had been more than he'd dreamed of.

"Morning." Shaun rolled over, more alert than Nathan had anticipated. "Merry Christmas."

"Merry Christmas to you too." Then Nathan closed the gap between them and kissed him lightly on the forehead. "How long have you been awake?"

"A while," Shaun admitted with a shrug.

"Why didn't you wake me up?"

Shaun smiled. "I was too busy enjoying listening to you breathing. I know that sounds weird, but… it felt good."

Nathan pushed him onto his back. "Now I want to enjoy looking at you."

Shaun bit his lip. "There's not much to look at. Not like you." He trailed his fingers over Nathan's shoulder, tracing a line down his bicep before tentatively stroking Nathan's chest.

Lord, that felt wonderful. Shaun's touch was light, almost reverential, a reminder—not that Nathan needed one—of his inexperience.

"Don't sell yourself short," Nathan remonstrated. "You're a good-looking man." He chuckled. "Momma called you skinny. Mind you, she couldn't see what I'm looking at."

"I'm not skinny," Shaun protested. "I'm blessed with good bone structure—got that from Mom—and I don't pile on the pounds—got that from Dad. I don't work out." He gave Nathan an inquiring glance. "You remember Dylan's other half, Mark? Now *there* is a guy who works out."

Nathan recalled him. "Mark's a handsome dude, I'll give you that, but…" He leaned over and kissed Shaun's chest. "He's not my type," he whispered.

Shaun's breathing caught. "You have a 'type'?"

Nathan nodded. "I like a funny, sweet guy with a lean body and eyes I could stare into all day. I like beards too, especially since I can't get mine to grow more than this fuzz you see here." He stroked his chin, then moved his hand over Shaun's chest, pausing to tease his nipple.

Shaun bit back a moan. "This is *not* a good idea."

"Why?"

He gave Nathan an incredulous stare. "We're in your momma's house. Walls have ears. And as if my morning wood wasn't a big enough problem, you have to make it worse?"

Nathan couldn't resist. He slid his hand beneath the comforter, encountering warm skin, inching lower until his fingertips met the soft cotton of Shaun's briefs.

He cupped the firm bulge, molding his fingers around Shaun's hard length. "Want some help with that?"

Shaun's breathing quickened. "What?"

"I'm in the same spot. So why don't we help each other out?" His own dick was doing a fair impression of a steel bar.

Shaun swallowed. "You know I've never…"

He stopped Shaun's words with a kiss. "I'm not gonna push you further than you're prepared to go, okay?"

"Okay." The breathless quality of Shaun's voice was turning him on.

"So… do you trust me?"

Shaun locked gazes with him, and the naked conviction he saw there made him tremble. "I trust you."

Nathan straddled Shaun's body, his weight on his hands, and inserted his legs between Shaun's. He gave a slow roll of his hips, brushing Shaun's erection with his own heavy shaft.

"Oh God," Shaun said with a groan.

"Want me to stop?"

Shaun glared at him. "Don't you dare."

Nathan smiled, then gave another leisurely roll. He pushed with his knees, spreading Shaun wide, and rocked up and down, nudging Shaun's sac, only this time, Shaun met him with movement of his own.

"That's it," Nathan praised. "Do what feels good."

Shaun's face was a mask of joy, his eyes sparkling as he nodded, his breathing quickening. Soon, his hands were on Nathan's ass, holding him firmly while he rocked his hips, a slow, sensual dry hump that sent Nathan's desire rocketing. He kissed Shaun's neck, breathing him in and nuzzling his warm skin. When they both picked up speed, Nathan figured it was time to change things a little.

He threw off the comforter and knelt between Shaun's spread thighs. "We need to lose these," he said, tugging at the waistband of Shaun's briefs. Shaun drew his knees to his chest, and Nathan slid the cotton over his firm ass, tossing the briefs to the floor. Then he removed his own. He yearned to spread those downy cheeks and spear his tongue into Shaun's hole, feeling it open for him, but he resisted the urge.

Shaun's right. Not now. But the time would come, of that Nathan was certain.

He straddled Shaun, wrapping his hand around both shafts and rolling his hips. Shaun's cut dick was flushed, his pubes tight and almost black around the root. His own cock was so dark against Shaun's, and he stared at the handful of stiff flesh, aware of Shaun's staccato breaths, heaving chest and quivering belly.

Shaun's hands were on his thighs, caressing him with that same gentle, reverential touch, his gaze fixed on Nathan's fingers curled around their solid lengths.

"Ready for more?" Nathan asked him, and he managed a nod. Nathan let go and resumed his previous position, propped up on his hands, only now their bare shafts met, hot and heavy. Nathan rocked against him, sliding his pre-cum-slicked length over Shaun's, shifting to rub his own balls over Shaun's sac. They moved together, Shaun writhing beneath him, hips in constant motion as he met Nathan's sensual frotting. He locked his arms around Nathan's neck, clinging to him as Nathan jerked his hips.

"Close," Shaun said with a gasp. "Feels… oh fuck, it feels so good. Don't want it to end."

Neither did Nathan. He picked up the pace, and to his mind, what they lacked in grace and rhythm, they made up for in fervent kisses, feeding each other moans as hot bare shafts collided over and over again, until they reached critical mass.

Shaun groaned, warmth trickled between them, and Nathan knew he wasn't far behind. He buried his face in Shaun's neck as he shot hard, trembling with each pulse of his dick. Shaun clung to him still, his breaths harsh in Nathan's ears, tremors spreading through him.

"Oh God." He cupped Nathan's head and kissed his cheeks, his forehead, his nose, lips, chin...Nathan returned his kisses, his torso sticky with their mingled cum. He shifted off Shaun's body and grabbed the box of tissues from the nightstand. Once all traces were wadded in handfuls of tissue, Nathan dropped them onto the rug. He grasped the comforter and hauled it over them, pulling Shaun into his arms.

"I thought I'd be getting chocolate or socks for Christmas," Nathan said with a smile. "This was way better."

Shaun took his hand and brought it to his lips. He kissed Nathan's fingers. "Not that I don't love my bracelet, but... yeah, I'd have to agree. This was way better." He glanced toward the door. "We didn't make too much noise, did we?"

Nathan chuckled. "Put it this way. If we did, we'll soon know."

The morning had given Shaun a glow he was positive anyone with half a brain could spot. He caught himself replaying the scene over and over again, recalling the feel of Nathan's body, the warmth of Nathan's bare cock rubbing against his. Then he'd glance at the faces of Nathan's family to check no one had caught him lost in his sensual recollections.

Either he wasn't as obvious as he thought he was, Nathan's momma and siblings were oblivious, or...

It was the *or* that bothered him most. *Or they know exactly what was going on, and they're saying nothing.*

Shaun was more aware of Nathan than ever. Each time they passed each other in the hallway, or when they sat together at the table or on the couch, he yearned to take Nathan's hand in his, to kiss him... That sprig of mistletoe was a pleasant reminder of his first kiss, but it taunted him.

Shaun wanted to be bold enough to kiss Nathan under its boughs once more.

The presents had all been opened and Jadyn had disposed of the wrapping paper. Christmas carols played in the background, and now and then, Cassie's voice rang out from the kitchen as she sang along. When 'Joy to the World' filled the air, Shaun smiled.

"This is my dad's favorite."

Then it hit him, as forceful as a blow to his solar plexus. Dad was gone, and for one tiny fragment of a moment, Shaun had forgotten that.

He choked out a sob, and Nathan's hand was on his back in a heartbeat. Shaun swiped at his cheeks, his throat tight.

"I gotcha," Nathan whispered. "It's okay."

But it *wasn't* okay. He didn't want to weep, not in front of Nathan's family. He wanted to keep a lid on his emotions, not let them pour out.

Phoebe left Kelsey on the rug and came over to sit beside Shaun. "If you feel like crying, then you cry, you hear me? Because you're not alone."

He jerked his head to stare at her.

Phoebe's eyes glistened. "That first night we had dinner, I took one look at Kelsey and Joey at their table, and I turned to ask my daddy if it brought back memories of when we were that little. And he's been gone a while now." She wiped away her tears with her fingers.

From the armchair, Jadyn nodded. "You'll find yourself seeing or hearing something, and you'll think, 'Oh, I gotta tell Dad about that.' I was doing that for *years*, long after Daddy passed."

"None of us expect you to be super-human," Phoebe said softly. "I'm amazed at how you've kept it all together so far."

"I thought I'd done all my crying," Shaun confessed. He felt wrung out.

Nathan stroked up and down his spine. "Not even close."

"You don't need to hide what you're feeling, not from us," Leo said warmly.

Then Shaun caught his breath when Nathan kissed his cheek. "Sounds like good advice to me," he murmured.

Shaun swore he'd have whiplash, he jerked his head so freaking fast. He gazed at Nathan, his heart racing. "We're not hiding?"

Nathan shook his head. "Nope." Then Shaun melted as Nathan's lips met his in a chaste kiss, accompanied by a chorus of *aws*.

"Hallelujah," Jadyn hollered. "Does Momma know?"

A cackle came from the doorway. "Course Momma knows. Momma knew before you did." Cassie came over to where Shaun sat, took his hands in hers, and pulled him to his feet before enveloping him in a hug. "I'm glad you like the sweater," she whispered, "but I think I got the better deal when it comes to presents."

He frowned. "I don't understand."

Cassie cupped his cheek. "You, sweetheart. You make my boy smile. Hell, you light him up like that Christmas tree over there."

Shaun couldn't hold back another second. He threw his arms around Cassie and hugged her so tightly that she let out a mock gasp. "You trying to crack my ribs?"

He laughed and released her. "Thank you. I think if I'd been at home, I'd have given Christmas a miss this year. That's two for two. You made Thanksgiving so special, and you made me feel so welcome in your home. All of you," he added, gazing at them.

Jadyn coughed. "Momma, if you're here, who's cooking?"

"I came in to say we're eating in half an hour, but just for that, you can help me." Cassie's eyes twinkled. "The rest of you can get the table ready." She raised her eyes heavenward to where the mistletoe hung. "Did it come in handy?"

Nathan chuckled. "You already know the answer to that, don't you?"

She beamed. "Then it was worth *almost* ending up in the Emergency Room." Her hips swinging, she left the room, humming a carol.

Shaun shook his head. "I'll say it again. Your momma is awesome." He grinned. "And I don't care what the rest of you think—I *love* her eggnog."

Jadyn gave a mock gasp. "Don't let this one go, Nathan. He's a keeper." When Nathan glanced at him, Jadyn cackled. "We can give Shaun our glasses of the stuff, instead of us coming up with fresh ideas for what to do with it."

Before Nathan could come back at him with a response, Shaun cleared his throat. "Hey, I can take one for the team, but I'm gonna insist on being paid."

Phoebe laughed. "How much do you charge?"

"You can pay me in kisses," Shaun said with a smile. Then he pointed to Nathan. "As long as *he's* the one who pays me."

Nathan's eyes gleamed. "I think we can work with that." He took Shaun's hand and drew him toward the rug. "How about a down payment?"

Amid whoops and hollers, Shaun lost himself in a slow, tender kiss. *I could* so *become addicted to this.*

He was already addicted to Nathan.

Chapter Nineteen

December 27

Nathan placed their bags into the trunk and closed it. All that was missing was Cat, and the furry little monster was doing a great job of evading capture. He'd gained a couple of new fans: Kelsey and Joey adored him, and during the last few days it had become commonplace to see Cat sitting with them, or in Joey's lap.

Shaun has gained some fans too. It delighted Nathan how his family had taken to Shaun, even if it meant they were making all kinds of assumptions.

Nathan wasn't assuming anything. It had only been a few days, and it didn't matter how badly he wanted to keep Shaun in his life—he hadn't talked to Shaun about that yet.

He stomped his feet on the doormat before entering the house. Phoebe came out of the living room, grinning. "I think you've lost something. Furry, soft paws, long swishy tail? You'd better grab Cat before Kelsey stuffs him in his bag and tries to sneak him into the car."

He gave her a hug. "You'll be a lot bigger next time I see you. When's your due date?"

Phoebe placed her hand on her belly. "It's going to be a midsummer baby."

"Are you gonna ask what the sex is at your twenty-week scan?"

She chuckled. "I keep forgetting my brother is a nurse. And yes, we'll ask. I'll be happy whatever we get, but Kelsey wants a little brother." She sighed. "It was so good to see you, but better than that, to see you happy."

"Hey, don't get ahead of yourself."

She held up her hands. "I'm trying, but every time I see the two of you, I think this is going to work out. Hold onto him, bro. He's special."

"You've noticed, huh?"

Shaun came out of the kitchen. "Is everything in the car?"

"Apart from Cat, yeah. He's avoiding capture."

Shaun smiled. "Leave him to me."

Nathan followed him into the living room, where Shaun placed the carrier on the rug, and knelt beside it.

"Come on, Cat."

To Nathan's surprise, Cat zipped out from under the table and zoomed across the room to Shaun, who scooped him into his arms and put him in the carrier.

Nathan gaped. "I've been trying to get him to do that for the last hour. How did you manage it in less than a minute?"

Shaun held up a little soft gray mouse. "Catnip. It was in that stocking full of cat Christmas treats you got him. I put another in the carrier too."

"Sneaky. I like it."

After a final round of goodbyes, it was just him, Shaun, and Momma in the hallway. She hugged Shaun tightly. "Come back soon, okay? There'll always be a bed here for you." Her eyes gleamed. "For both of you. As long as you won't mind sharing again."

Nathan snorted. "Momma, making us share like that? *Not* subtle."

She chuckled. "No, son. 'Not subtle' would've been making you share—and not putting a foldaway in there." She hugged Nathan. "Don't stay away too long, you hear?"

"I won't, I promise."

"And I'll make sure he sticks to that promise," Shaun added. He glanced at Nathan with a smile.

Warmth spread through him. Maybe it was safe to make a few assumptions after all.

Shaun opened the front door and stepped into the cool interior. It wasn't just the temperature that sent a shiver through him, but the emptiness of the place. Compared with the color and glitter of Christmas at Cassie's, the house seemed drab.

"You don't have to go right away, do you?" he asked Nathan. After four days of chatter and laughter, he wasn't sure he was ready for solitude.

Nathan smiled. "No, I can stay a while. But I might let Cat out though, and feed him. I'll take him into the kitchen." In one hand he held the pet carrier, and in the other, a couple of bulging plastic bags. "Momma must think you need feeding too. I swear she gave you most of the Christmas leftovers."

"As if I'm gonna complain about having more of Cassie's cooking."

Nathan coughed. "I think I need to come over for dinner a few nights this week. To help you eat it all, I mean." He went through the archway to the kitchen.

I hope that's not the only reason. Then he pushed such thoughts aside. *How could I even think that, after the Christmas we just shared?*

Shaun knelt on the rug in front of the fire. Thankfully, there were enough logs in the basket to mean he didn't need to go outside into the cold. He set up the kindling and twists of newspaper, then lit them. By the time Nathan returned, the kindling was glowing red, flames licking their way through the pile of sticks and pieces of soft wood.

"I've stowed everything in the fridge." Nathan knelt beside him. "Did you have a good time?"

Shaun nodded. "Apart from this morning. I hope Cassie gets her boiler fixed. The whole house was as cold as a witch's tit when we woke up." The fire in the living room had helped, and everyone had gathered in there. A cozy start to the day, huddled around the fire, eating oatmeal.

Nathan grinned. "You didn't feel like a cold shower then."

He shuddered. "Hell no, but I might grab one now." Shaun peered at Nathan. "Will you stay until I'm done?"

Nathan leaned in and kissed him. "Will you relax? I'll still be here when you get out of the shower. I'll turn up the heat, and I'll add logs to the fire. Now go."

Shaun expelled a sigh. "Thank you." He got up from the floor and headed for his room. Less than five minutes later, he was standing under a steady stream of hot water, head bowed, hands flat to the tiled wall, trying not to think about how fucking *needy* he'd sounded. Okay, so the prospect of being alone made his stomach clench. He'd *been* alone after Dad died, hadn't he? Why did this feel so different?

Because then he'd known Nathan would be around, but when Monday arrived, Nathan would be back to his job and Shaun would be in the restaurant—and coming home to a house with no Dad.

Shaun came out of the bathroom, a towel around his waist. He gazed at the discarded clothing on the bed, and his heartbeat shifted into a higher gear. He dropped the towel and grabbed his robe from the hook on the door. As he fastened it around him, an idea stole into his mind, one that made his heart beat even faster, and he yanked open the nightstand drawer.

Just in case.

He went back to the living room where the fire blazed, its warmth spilling into every corner of the room. Nathan sat on the rug, staring into the flames and smiling.

"What are you thinking about?" Shaun asked on impulse.

Nathan turned to look at him. "This morning."

Shaun joined him on the rug, his arms wrapped around his knees, his robe covering all of him. "Before or after we got up?"

"Before." Nathan's eyes sparkled in the firelight. "'Warm me up', you said. And we certainly got warm."

Shaun's heated face had nothing to do with the fire, and everything to do with the recollection of his hand around Nathan's thick cock. "You know what was hardest about staying at your momma's house?"

Nathan's lips twitched. "Yeah. Pretty sure I had it in my hand this morning."

Shaun coughed. "I didn't mean that—although you have a point. I was talking about keeping quiet." Not to mention the illicit thrill that at any moment, Cassie might've knocked on their door.

"We don't have to be quiet anymore," Nathan said in a low voice. "Because now there's just us."

A shiver slid up and down Shaun's spine. "I was thinking the same thing all the way here. Well, about that… and other things."

Nathan stilled, his gaze locked on Shaun's. "Care to share your thoughts?"

He took a deep breath. "Just because I have no experience, doesn't mean I haven't… imagined what it would be like. I've imagined a lot."

Nathan smiled. "Of course you have. I wouldn't expect anything else."

"And I *have* watched a bit of porn," Shaun added.

Nathan cocked his head. "Straight porn? Or gay?"

"Gay. Not that I let the others know."

"But why not?"

Shaun wasn't sure he could explain his reasons. "It wasn't important, all right? Dad was my life. I could've dated after Mom died, before he started getting worse, but… it felt wrong." He gazed into the fire. "Sex didn't figure in my list of priorities. I made do with my hand, and a little porn now and then when I wanted to get out of my head." He gestured to the room. "Out of here. But I always knew I was into guys, not girls."

"I'm in the same boat as you. Porn has been a substitute for a guy in my bed for a long while now. And while we're on the subject…" Nathan cleared his throat. "I know you told me about Dylan's boyfriend, but it kinda went in one ear and out the other. So when I met your friends at the funeral, I think I did an awesome job of not reacting. I kept looking at Mark and thinking 'Where do I know you from?' Then it hit me."

"Oh. You've seen his... work?" Shaun had deliberately avoided any Mark Roman videos that crossed his path. That would've been plain wrong.

Nathan chuckled. "Yeah. Hard to stand around after a funeral and chat with someone when you've seen them naked and getting busy with a bunch of guys."

He couldn't resist a quick poke. "You're talking to me, and you've seen *me* naked."

Nathan's smile sent heat trickling through him. "Yeah, and I want to see more of you." He cupped Shaun's cheek. "A *lot* more." Then he trailed his fingers down Shaun's neck before sliding them beneath his robe. "Now would be a good time."

Shaun's breath caught as Nathan untied the belt around Shaun's waist, and then pushed his robe off his shoulders, baring his torso. "What did you have in mind?" he whispered as Nathan bent to kiss his shoulder.

Nathan raised his head to meet Shaun's gaze. "I leave that part up to you."

He blinked. "Me?"

Nathan nodded. "You call the shots." He planted another gentle kiss on Shaun's neck, moving lower to kiss along his collarbone, and each intimate gesture sent a thrill skittering through him.

"Nathan..." Shaun couldn't think straight.

"I mean it. You're in charge here. Tell me what you want." He smiled. "The time for imagining is over.

Now you get to make it a reality."

He shuddered as Nathan brushed his lips over Shaun's nipple. "I want to… kiss you… touch you…" Shaun traced a line down Nathan's body, until his fingertips grazed the bulge at his crotch. "I want this too." Nathan straightened, and Shaun stepped out of his comfort zone. "Inside me." *Oh God.* Nathan's shaft, filling him, stretching him…

"You sure? We don't have to."

Shaun went with the truth. "I came to the conclusion a while back, long before I'd even met you." He smiled. "I've always wanted to be the slot for someone's tab."

Nathan regarded him in silence for a moment, and Shaun ached to know what he was thinking. "I'm more of a tab kinda guy myself."

Relief surged through him. "Perfect."

"But before we go any further, can I play nurse for a second?"

"Okay."

"If you're gonna bottom, then we need to discuss—"

"Do we need condoms?" Shaun blurted.

Nathan arched his eyebrows. "Something else you've been thinking about?"

He nodded. "I mean, I'm a virgin…"

Nathan chuckled. "Correction. You *were* a virgin, before you came in my hand this morning. And on me on Christmas Day." Shaun opened his mouth to speak, but Nathan continued. "I have my regular physicals, and I haven't been with anyone in a long time."

"So what you're saying is, we're both good to go?" Shaun's pulse quickened. "Because I want you inside me, nothing between us. Is that okay?"

Nathan smiled. "I didn't really want to go out condom-hunting on a Sunday night, not if I could help it. But we'll still need lube."

Shaun reached into the pocket of his robe and removed the bottle. "Surprise."

Nathan took it from him and set it aside. "We don't need that just yet." He removed his sweater, then the tee beneath it, and Shaun couldn't help but admire the tautness of his belly, the wide chest, how Nathan's body seemed to glow in the firelight, as if he'd oiled it.

"You have lovely skin," he murmured. Then he held his breath as Nathan undid his jeans and got up to remove them. He stood before Shaun, naked and beautiful, his dick long and heavy, rising to meet Shaun's lips. Shaun placed his hands on Nathan's hips, and kissed the wide head of Nathan's cock.

Nathan expelled a soft sigh. "Oh, that's so nice." He cupped Shaun's head, stroking his hair as Shaun took the head into his mouth, flicking it with his tongue, savoring its smoothness and inhaling the musky odor that hardened his own dick.

Nathan lifted Shaun's chin with his fingers. "I want to take my time with you. Is that okay?"

Shaun smiled. "I'm in no hurry to get anywhere. I just wanna enjoy the journey." He'd waited long enough for this trip, he wanted it to last.

Nathan's hands were gentle as he spread Shaun's robe on the rug, then pushed him onto his back. Nathan covered him with his body, and their lips met. Shaun lost track of time as they kissed, his hands on Nathan's shoulders and nape. Skin touched skin, and that connection remained unbroken as they rocked against each other, Nathan's cock hard against his own,

Shaun's knees drawn up, his legs spread. When that first slick finger penetrated him, he moaned into Nathan's kiss, thankful for the pause as Nathan stilled inside him.

"You're so warm in there," Nathan murmured against his lips. "So tight. Feels good." He looked Shaun in the eyes. "And we don't go any further until it feels good for you too."

Shaun captured Nathan's sweet face and pulled him down into a fervent kiss, a catch in his breathing as Nathan began to move with a leisurely in and out motion.

It was nothing like he'd imagined. Naked on the rug, the fire warming them, Nathan explored him with a gentleness that almost overwhelmed him. And when Shaun declared himself ready for more, Nathan moved him onto his side facing the fire, raised Shaun's leg to hook it over his own, and guided his cock into position.

Nathan kissed him as he slowly entered him, his hand cradling Shaun's head. Shaun moaned into the kiss as Nathan's cock stretched him, breathing though the burn until it morphed into something more pleasurable. And once Shaun's body fully sheathed his dick, Nathan held him close, stroking his chest as he kissed Shaun's mouth, cheeks, and neck.

Shaun didn't know which created more warmth—the fire spilling heat over his body, or the delicious friction of Nathan's shaft sliding in and out. And when Nathan rolled him carefully onto his back, his cock deep inside Shaun as he rested Shaun's legs against his broad shoulders, Shaun gave himself up to the exquisite sensations. Nathan rocked into him, and Shaun clung to him, his heart pounding, his breath harsh and loud in the quiet room. They found their rhythm, moving together, and Shaun felt slick skin beneath his fingers. His own chest was damp with sweat, his body tingled, and with each glide of Nathan's dick inside him, Nathan brought them closer to the end.

"Love this," Shaun whispered as Nathan buried his face in Shaun's neck, hips rolling, Shaun wrapped in his arms, held secure. Shaun curled his fingers around his own cock and worked it, groaning into Nathan's kiss as the sensations heightened. And when he shot, warmth pooling on his belly, Nathan kissed him through his climax, whispering into his ear how beautiful he was when he came.

Then it was Nathan's turn. His face was inches from Shaun's as he rocked faster, their gazes locked on one another, and Shaun knew he was close. Nathan stilled, and the throbbing within him filled him with fierce exultation. He wound his fingers in Nathan's mass of curls, drawing him close to kiss him as Nathan shuddered, aware of the pulsing inside him.

Nathan lay on top of him, Shaun's legs wrapped around his waist. "Oh, you amazing man," he said breathlessly.

Shaun couldn't hold back his smile. "Me? You did all the work."

Nathan kissed the tip of his nose. "That's okay. Next time, you're gonna ride me."

Next time... Two little words that sent Shaun's heart soaring.

The tick of the clock on the mantelpiece was an unwelcome intrusion. Nathan eased out of him, then kissed him softly. "Don't be surprised if you're a little sore."

"It'll pass, right?" Shaun swallowed. "Do you have to go?"

Nathan shook his head. "I'll stay tonight. I need to be up early tomorrow though."

Shaun's stomach gave a growl. "How about we get cleaned up, then eat some of Cassie's leftovers?" There were still a few hours before bed.

"Sounds good to me." Nathan swiped his fingers over Shaun's chest and grinned. "*Someone* needs another shower."

"Think we can both fit in there?" He was only delaying the inevitable, he knew that, but he didn't want to lose this connection.

More than that, he didn't want to lose Nathan. He *couldn't*.

"You wash my back, and I'll wash yours." Nathan's eyes sparkled. "But no getting frisky in the shower. I don't want to have to tell Momma how we ended up in the ER. I'd never hear the last of it."

"Can I at least kiss you?"

Nathan pressed his lips to Shaun's forehead. "That much, I was planning on doing."

Shaun didn't think he could live without Nathan's kisses.

Who am I kidding? Right then he didn't believe he could live without Nathan.

Chapter Twenty

December 30

Shaun got behind the wheel and put his keys into the ignition. It was a relief to get out of the icy blast that had whipped its way through Portland as he'd hurried to the Fore Street garage. Nathan had messaged to say he'd be over later, but that he wouldn't be staying.

Even his text had sounded tired. Shaun got that part all too well.

The joy of Christmas had been banished to the past: reality was in, and it was kicking Shaun's ass. Not that he could complain—the present situation was partly his own fault. He'd gone back to work Monday, and when Sandy had mentioned they'd be open all week, Shaun had asked for—and gotten—extra hours. The restaurant had never been busier. It seemed as if everyone in Portland wanted to eat out after a weekend of family and festive food.

With one day left before New Year's, Shaun was ready for a break. He hadn't given a moment's thought to his birthday, but then, he hadn't done that for the last seven or so years. Levi's text that morning to confirm Shaun and Nathan would be at the party had served as a reminder: for the first time, he wasn't going alone, and the realization brought with it a slew of mixed emotions.

Shaun was so *torn*.

He hadn't seen much of Nathan since their return Sunday, but that was down to Shaun's hours, and it being a difficult time of year for many seniors: Nathan was coping with more work due to a bout of the flu that was hitting everyone, in-home nurses included, and more patients requiring help. And although Nathan dropped by after work, his brief visits were a two-edged sword.

There were only so many times Shaun could reply to Nathan's *How are you?* with *I'm fine.* Easy words to say when he was anything but fine. He should've shared what was on his mind, he knew that, but instead he'd gone with kissing on the couch.

Anything to avoid conversation.

New Year's brought with it the prospect of change. He'd meant it when he'd told Nathan's family he was considering going back to school, but up till the present moment, they had been mere words.

Maybe I need to look into it. At least he knew someone who could advise him.

Shaun got his phone out and composed a brief text to Finn. *You available for a chat later?*

Finn's reply was almost instantaneous. *What's wrong with now?*

He smiled as he hit Call. "What's wrong is that I'm sitting in my car, freezing my butt off. I was gonna call you when I got home and thawed out."

"Does this have to be a voice call, or can I visit?"

That stopped him in his tracks. The guys had never been to the house, apart from after the funeral, a result of Shaun's desire to keep his two worlds separate.

Maybe it was time to change that too.

"Only if you're sure. I mean, I hate to drag you

out of a nice warm house—and away from Joel."

Finn chuckled. "Joel has gone to see Carrie and the kids. Laura got a puppy for Christmas, and Joel's taking Bramble along to add to the mayhem."

"Didn't you wanna go too?"

"To be honest? I was enjoying having the place to myself. We had a houseful last weekend. I've had a quiet afternoon reading, and I was just about to heat up some soup."

"Want pizza instead? I'm starving." He could've grabbed something at work, but by the time eight o'clock had rolled around, Shaun just wanted out of there.

"Ooh, I can do that. I'll buy. Pepperoni work for ya? I'll pick it up on the way, as soon as I put your address into my GPS. I can't remember the way to your place. Joel was driving when we came to the funeral, and I wasn't really paying attention."

Relief swamped him. "That'd be awesome. It's easy to spot my house—look for the one without Christmas lights." He chuckled. "Just call me Ebeneezer Scrooge."

Finn cackled. "Gotcha. Google says it'll take me thirty-five minutes. Just goes to show Google knows diddly squat about snow-covered roads."

He chuckled. "Then I'd better get my ass home. See you soon." He disconnected, then switched on the engine, his heart lighter.

By the time Finn's truck pulled onto the driveway, the fire had a healthy supply of logs, and the living room was as warm as toast. He opened the door to find Finn stomping his boots to shake off the snow, and took the proffered box that instantly filled the room with a heavenly aroma.

"Coat off, boots off, and go sit by the fire."

Finn gazed at his surroundings as he removed his outer wear. "This is such a pretty room. I love the bookcases framing the window." Then he lurched across the floor to the fireplace. "I think I've spent most of the winter so far in an armchair next to the fire. I'm turning into my grandfather." He sat on the couch, stretching his hands toward the flames.

"You want a plate, or are we gonna be slobs and eat it from the box?"

Finn's eyes sparkled. "Slobs. Too hungry to wait for plates. I got a large. That okay?" Shaun's stomach grumbled, and Finn laughed. "I'm guessing that's a yes."

For the next ten minutes neither of them spoke as they got down to the all-important business of devouring the pizza. Both sagged against the seat cushions when the box contained nothing but a smear of grease.

"I needed that," Shaun admitted. "What do you want to drink? There's coffee, tea, hot chocolate, soda…"

"You got any decaf?"

Shaun smiled. "That, I can do." He took the pizza box into the kitchen, and reached into a cabinet for the jar of decaf.

Finn followed him, stopping in the doorway. "This is a cute house. You always lived here?"

He nodded. "They thought about moving when it was time for me to go to school. Mom liked the look of Wells for a while there, but they decided moving *and* starting school was too big an upheaval, so they stayed put, and I took the bus." He filled the kettle. "Nathan asked if I wanted to sell this place. I don't think I could, you know? Okay, for the last few years it felt less like a home, but that was because Mom was gone, and Dad was… well, you know the rest. But it could be a home again."

Finn cleared his throat. "Your text… was there a reason why you wanted to talk to me?"

"Actually, yeah. I want to pick your brains."

Finn snorted. "Haven't you heard? I do construction. We don't have brains, only enough intelligence to wield a hammer, and jeans that slip constantly to reveal our asses. Intentionally, of course." He grinned. "What's up?"

Shaun told him about his dad's letter, and the suggestion that he could make changes in his life if he so wished. "There *was* one route I was considering, but I wanted to talk to you about it first."

"Color me intrigued."

"Do you think I'm too old to go back to school to learn how to be a carpenter like you?"

Finn blinked. "Really?"

"Well, carpenter, joiner, working with wood…" He smiled. "I like the idea of working with my hands, making something."

Finn rubbed his chin. "Okay," he enunciated slowly. "Let's deal with your question. No, you're never too old to learn something new." Shaun beamed, and Finn held up his hands. "But before you start filling in application forms for Southern Maine Community College, can I make a suggestion?"

"That's why I wanted to talk to you. I figured you'd have some ideas."

Finn nodded. "What kind of hours are you working at the restaurant?"

"Usually about thirty hours a week, but I *could*

work less." He wouldn't have to worry about money, not once the insurance people paid up.

"Then how about this? After New Year's—and a change in the weather—why don't you go part-time? The rest of the week, come and work with me. You'd be my general laborer, mind you, and I wouldn't take it easy on you. This is so you have a realistic idea of what it would be like."

Shaun let out a sigh. "That sounds perfect. Yes, please. When can I start?"

Finn laughed. "Well, there's a reason I'm not working right now. It's called snow. You might have seen some of it around. When things warm up a bit, *then* we'll start. I'm in the middle of building a house in Ogunquit. The guy bought a dilapidated house, tore it down, and got someone to design him a new one. I'd gotten as far as putting up the frame before the real heavy snows hit."

Shaun handed him a cup of coffee. "Let's head back to the fire." They went into the living room and Shaun grabbed his favorite spot on the rug.

"This is nice," Finn said as he joined him. "I keep telling Joel he needs a rug in front of the fireplace. Perfect for cold winter nights." When Shaun coughed, Finn arched his eyebrows. "Coffee went down the wrong way?"

"Something like that, yeah." What came to mind was Nathan on his back on the rug, Shaun riding him like he was John fucking Wayne, hips bucking, both of them working up a sweat.

"So… what's the deal with Nathan?" Finn's casual tone didn't fool Shaun for a second.

"What do you mean?"

Finn drank some more before speaking. "I

mean, when both Levi *and* Ben insisted we leave an empty seat next to yours at the funeral, and then practically shoved Nathan onto it, I know *something* is going on."

Shaun took a deep breath. "That would be because something is." He fell silent, his gaze locked on the fire. When Finn didn't respond, Shaun glanced at him.

Finn's jaw had dropped. "You little... Seriously?" Shaun nodded, and Finn's face erupted into a beaming smile. "Oh, that's awesome news. Really. I can't tell you how happy that makes me." Then his smile faded. "Except that's not all, is it? There's something else."

Shaun put his cup down on the hearth. "Don't get me wrong. What we've shared so far has been *beyond* amazing. But..."

Finn's hand covered his. "It's okay. If you wanna talk about it, I'm a good listener. And if you don't, that's fine too." He cocked his head to one side. "But I get the feeling you do." He withdrew his hand.

"Yeah. I have to tell someone." He scowled at the flickering flames. "I'm my own worst enemy, you know that?"

"What does that mean?"

Shaun took a moment to frame his fears. "He's come to mean so much to me in a relatively short time. I've even found myself fantasizing about him being a permanent part of my life. Waking up to see his face on the pillow next to mine. But... what if I'm seeing it all wrong? What if none of this is real?"

Finn's brow furrowed. "You're gonna have to explain that."

Shaun expelled a sigh. "What if the only reason

I have feelings for Nathan... the only reason I latched onto him... was because he was the only one there for me? What if that has... skewed my view of this relationship?" He ran his fingers through his hair. "See what I mean? I don't even know if what I'm feeling is real."

Finn's soft sigh echoed his. "Sounds to me as if you're very self-aware, but I think you're missing something important."

"Yeah?" Shaun gave him an inquiring gaze. "You gonna share?"

"How does Nathan make you feel?"

He stared at Finn, perplexed.

"Okay, let's come at this from another angle. Do you think about him when he's not here?"

"Yes."

"Do you look forward to seeing him?"

"Yes." Shaun counted the hours.

"Does the thought of him give you the warm fuzzies?"

He smiled. "Is that a technical term?"

"You know what I mean. Does he make you happy?"

Oh God, yes. "Yes."

Finn smiled. "Sounds to me like you love him. Sounds to *me* as if you're imagining a life with Nathan because that's what you really want." His eyes twinkled. "So how does he feel about you?"

Shaun didn't think Nathan was the kind of guy to take him to spend Christmas with his momma and family if there weren't some serious feelings at play. Then again, Cassie had kinda insisted, right? And hadn't it been her idea, not Nathan's?

Finn's smile hadn't faded. "There's only one

surefire way of knowing that. The two of you need to talk. That's one thing I've learned from being with Joel—when you have something on your mind, the best thing to do is bring it out into the open. Two heads really are better than one, and bottling stuff up only makes you miserable." He cocked his head toward the door. "You expecting someone?"

Shaun rolled his eyes. "I think you already know the answer to that." Outside, a car engine died.

Finn got to his feet. "Perfect timing. This is my cue to leave."

Shaun stood. "Thanks for coming over, and for the pizza. And the straight talk."

Finn grinned. "A word which apparently applies to neither of us." He shook his head. "And I thought we were done with surprises for this year. You both coming to Levi's tomorrow night?"

"That's the plan."

Finn hugged him. "Then talk tonight. Start the New Year with a clear mind. Decide what you want and go for it."

The front door opened, and Nathan stepped inside. He smiled when he saw Finn. "Hey. It's Finn, isn't it?"

"Yeah, but I was just leaving. I'll be at the party though."

"Oops. Lemme move my car. I'm blocking you in." He dashed out into the snow.

Finn gave Shaun another hug. "Good luck. See you tomorrow." He followed Nathan out into the cold night air.

Shaun knelt by the fire and added another couple of logs. When Nathan returned, he indicated the rug. "Wanna help yourself to coffee, then join me?"

Nathan's dark eyes gleamed. "What do you have in mind?"

Shaun seized his courage with both hands. "A talk."

Chapter Twenty-One

Finally. Nathan hadn't been able to shake the feeling all week that something was coming. "Will coffee do, or do I need something stronger?" He joined Shaun on the rug, wrapping his arms around his knees.

"I don't think so."

Thank God. Nathan studied him, the firelight casting a warm glow on Shaun's face. "Then what's wrong?"

"Have you eaten? I can make you a sandwich, or—" He moved as if to stand, and Nathan grabbed his arm.

"You're staying right where you are until you've told me what's on your mind."

Shaun pushed out a long breath. "Okay. You know I've been working a lot this week. We both have." Nathan nodded. "Well, what I didn't mention was... I asked for those extra hours."

"Why?"

"I was avoiding this place. I guess I haven't gotten used to coming home to an empty house."

Nathan's heart went out to him. "Why didn't you call me? I would've been here ASAP." When Shaun didn't respond, Nathan's stomach clenched. "Unless you didn't want me around." Except his gut told him Shaun would've said something if that had been the case.

Shaun gazed into the fire. "I've been telling

myself I need to stand on my own two feet. That I can't keep relying on you."

Nathan loved Shaun's desire to be strong, but he had to fight the urge to yell that it was too soon. *He's still wrapped up in grief.* "And if I *want* you to rely on me? Hmm?" *Dear Lord.* Nathan would do anything to help Shaun shoulder the burden he carried.

"It's not just that," Shaun protested.

"What else?"

"I guess I started doubting my emotions." He flushed. "I thought maybe I was reading too much into... something."

"Into what?" When Shaun didn't reply, Nathan stretched his arm out and cupped Shaun's chin, exerting gentle pressure until Shaun looked him in the eye. "Tell me."

"Into the... sex."

What the... Nathan blinked. "Explain, please?"

"It's not so difficult to understand. You're the first guy I've ever been... physical with. So I thought maybe... maybe what I was feeling for you was because of that. But it wasn't just that. I was getting ahead of myself, picturing a life with you in it—permanently. And that felt... selfish."

Oh, you sweet, sweet man.

Nathan withdrew his fingers, then shifted closer, tugging Shaun into his lap, his thighs hooking over Nathan's. "*You* are the least selfish man I've ever met. Let me share a few truths with you. I've worked with a lot of patients these last few years, people who were terminal, like Peter. I got to see their families too, and I gotta tell you, I felt sorry for some of the people I was caring for. All their families wanted was to go out and leave them to me. They didn't give a shit. Then I met you." He stroked Shaun's cheek. "In all the time I've known you, what impressed me most was how you always put your dad first, and your own happiness last." He leaned in and kissed Shaun on the lips, cradling the back of Shaun's head in his hands. "You've been selfless for so many years, but now's the time to change that. You deserve someone in your life who supports you, wants you… loves you…"

Shaun's eyes widened. "Loves me?"

"Oops. I guess I let the cat out of the bag." After weeks of holding back, Nathan was more than ready to bare his soul. He smiled. "It's not hard to love someone like you. And the more I got to know you, the more convinced I became that I could fall in love with you. I fought that feeling for so long, but now I'm done fighting. I've given up, and accepted that God has seen fit to bring a wonderful man into my life. And you *are* a wonderful man." He kissed Shaun again. "You're special. Every single person in my family could see that. Hell, Momma saw that at Thanksgiving. So I guess what I need to know is… this life you keep picturing with me in it… wanna make it a reality?"

"You mean it?"

Nathan didn't miss the note of hope in his voice. "You've watched your friends find love and romance, and you've cheered them on. Well, now it's your turn. You deserve all the love and romance I can give you. Just be prepared—I've got a lot to give. If you'll let me."

Come on, baby. Grab onto this new life I'm offering you.
Shaun deserved this. They both did.

Shaun was glad he was sitting down, because he felt certain his knees would've buckled and he'd have ended up flat on his ass.

He loves me.

I'm not delusional.

It's real.

Joy bubbled through him, and he wanted to shout from the roof.

"Unless you don't *want* to date me," Nathan added. "If that's the case, better tell me now. Gotta say though, I think I'm quite a catch." His lips twitched.

"You are," Shaun agreed. "Personally, I think I'd be getting the better deal."

"How do you work that out?"

Shaun held up his wrist, around which was his leather bracelet. "You gave me this for Christmas, and what did I give you? Chocolate." He'd wanted to give Nathan something special, but time had been short, and inspiration lacking.

"But you gave me so much more than chocolate." Nathan smiled. "I woke up Christmas morning with you in my bed, in my arms. You have *no* idea how long I'd dreamed of that. I swear I had bruises from pinching myself. And you haven't answered my question."

Warmth spread through his body in a slow tide. "You in my life? I'd be a fool to say no."

"Then let's take it slow, okay? No one is

suggesting we move in together next week, or live in each other's pockets 24/7. You were right about one thing. You've gone through a lot these past months. Give yourself time to adapt. But be sure of one thing—I'm not going anywhere."

Shaun looped his arms around Nathan's neck. "You're wrong, you know." When Nathan gave him a quizzical glance, Shaun smiled. "You'll be going home to feed Cat."

Nathan grinned. "Did that before I came here. I'm yours for the night." He stroked Shaun's beard. "And for all the nights to come."

"Love you," he whispered.

Nathan's smile reached his eyes. "Two words, and you just turned my world upside down. I love you too, and now I'm gonna show you just how much."

Shaun undid the top buttons of Nathan's shirt. "Show me here."

Nathan chuckled. "One of these nights we'll make it to your bed."

December 31

Shaun found a space for the car and backed into it. "You sure you want to drive us home?"

Nathan nodded. "I'll have a drink at midnight, but that's it. Besides, I don't expect you to go home sober. It's your birthday."

It had been the best birthday ever. From

morning cuddles—and everything that followed—to breakfast in bed, Nathan had made the whole day special.

"My birthday always takes second place at Levi and Grammy's New Year's Eve party, but I'm used to that." It didn't matter. Nothing could take the shine off Shaun's day. He was about to meet all his friends with a gorgeous man at his side. There'd be comments, but Shaun was ready for them.

I might even have a few comments of my own.

He knew what had brought about his change in mood. There was a new lightness to his heart, and a spring in his step, and all of it was down to Nathan. Thoughts of his dad were never far away, however, and he'd sat on the couch holding Dad's photo.

You were right, Dad. Nathan's a good guy. And he'll take good care of me, just like I'll take good care of him.

Nathan nudged him. "You think we could get out of the car now? I hear there's a party going on around here."

He chuckled. "Sorry. I zoned out for a second." They got out, Shaun locked the car, and they walked along the white picket fence that marked out Grammy's yard. Music came from inside, and Shaun glimpsed balloons and banners through the window. Before he could ring the bell, the door opened, and Levi greeted them with a beaming smile.

"Hey. Come on in." As they crossed the threshold, Levi extended a hand to Nathan. "Glad you could make it. A word of warning. Grammy's made hot rum punch, and it's not for the faint-hearted. Sip it."

Nathan laughed. "Thanks for the advice."

They removed their coats, and Levi hung them on the already burdened hooks. "You're the last ones to arrive. This year, it's just us," he told them. "And yes, there'll be fireworks at midnight."

"Who drew the short straw to light them this year while everyone else watches from indoors where it's warm?" Shaun asked.

"Noah. He's been bitching about it for the last hour. I told him, I did it last year. *And* the year before."

Shaun led Nathan to the door of the living room. "Ready?"

Nathan grinned. "Bring it on." He held out his hand, and Shaun took it. "Think this'll be a big enough hint?"

Levi stared at their joined hands. His gaze stuttered back to their faces, and he gasped. "Shaun Clark, you sneaky little…" Then he preened. "I guess pointing out how hot Nathan is gave you ideas, huh?"

Nathan stared at Shaun. "And when was this?"

Before Shaun could reply, Levi hugged the air out of his lungs. "So freakin' happy for you, dude," he whispered. Then Nathan got the same treatment. "You've got yourself one of the best. You take care of him, y'hear?"

Nathan smiled. "I know it, and you can be sure I will."

"Did they change their minds and go home?" Seb yelled from the other side of the door. Laughter followed.

"Uh-oh. Someone's getting impatient." Levi pushed them through the door, and a chorus of 'Happy Birthday' rang out. Above the mantelpiece was a colorful banner emblazoned with the words *Happy Birthday Shaun*, and everyone blew noisemakers. Finn led the assault of party poppers, joined by Joel and Ben, showering Shaun with confetti.

"What the—" Shaun gaped. "What's going on?"

"We decided it was about time we threw you a birthday party," Levi explained. "Actually, it was Grammy's idea."

Grammy got up from her chair by the fire, her arms wide. "Good timing. I was just about to go into the kitchen. Get over here and gimme a hug." Shaun didn't hesitate, and she held him tight. "Happy birthday, sweetheart, and many more." She let him go, peering around him. "Nathan, welcome."

"Thank you."

"Be sure to try my punch. It'll put hairs on your chest." Then she headed for the door.

Shaun stared after her with a mock glare. "But I don't *want* hairs on his chest. I like it just the way it is."

Silence fell for a moment, and then Seb cackled. "Something you wanna tell us, Shaun?"

"There's plenty of time for that. Let them be," Finn hollered.

"Oh, so there *is* a 'them', is there? And how come *you* knew about this and I didn't?" Seb put his hands on his hips.

"Maybe they didn't want it broadcast all over Maine?" Marcus suggested.

Seb narrowed his gaze. "You saying I've got a big mouth?"

Marcus grinned. "God, yes, sweetheart, and I love what you do with it."

Shaun fucking *loved* these guys.

Ben cackled. "Is there ever gonna be a shindig where we just get together and *no one* springs a surprise partner on us? Dear *Lord*, this is certainly a year to remember."

Aaron scowled. "Hey, what gives? The end of

the year, and I'm suddenly a minority?"

"You're not the only one," Noah complained. Then his eyes widened. "Hey, wait a minute. This means we've gone from eight to thirteen. There can't be thirteen of us. That's bad luck."

"Wait until Easter. Or Valentine's." Wade chuckled. "The way things have been going, anything could happen." His eyes sparkled. "Which of you, Aaron, and Levi is gonna take the plunge?"

Aaron folded his arms. "Well, don't look at me, 'cause *I'm* not looking."

Levi grinned. "Oh, you've done it now. Haven't you learned anything from the past nine months?" He pointed to the couples in the room. "None of *them* were looking, but it didn't matter. Love snuck up on 'em and hit 'em over the head with a baseball bat." His gaze met Shaun's. "And I fucking *love* it."

Nathan leaned in to Shaun. "That was easy," he said in a low voice.

Shaun snorted. "Don't relax yet. We only just got here."

And the night was young.

Midnight was less than fifteen minutes away, and Shaun was having a great time. One by one, his friends had given him a hug, and told him in a whisper that he had great taste. Nathan had gotten along like a house on fire with Marcus, Joel, and Mark, and it lifted

Shaun's heart to see the welcome Nathan had received.

Grammy had taken Nathan aside for a moment, and Shaun had wondered what the hell that was about. When Nathan returned, he was smiling.

"Did she want to give you her recipe for hot punch, or ask for a consultation about her varicose veins?"

Nathan leaned in. "She wanted me to know what a special man you were, and that if I didn't treat you right, she'd take a switch to my butt." He chuckled. "You were right. She's quite a character."

Even Grammy was looking out for him.

"Your friends are amazing," Nathan commented. "They've gone out of their way to make me feel at home." He smiled. "And I really do feel comfortable around them."

Yet another reason why Shaun couldn't stop smiling. He'd always known his friends were an enlightened bunch, and to have his belief in them confirmed brought him joy.

"There's still plenty of food, folks," Grammy hollered. "And make sure you fill your glasses before midnight."

Shaun patted Nathan's arm. "I'll go get us something."

Nathan gazed at him with wide eyes. "Where do you put it all?"

"I told you. Blame that on Dad."

Grammy turned on the TV and changed channels. New York was gearing up for the dropping of the red ball. His throat tightened. *First time in forever that I don't share a midnight toast with Dad.* Then he glanced at Nathan, and the compassion in those dark brown eyes almost unraveled him.

I know, Nathan mouthed.

Shaun got himself under control again, and joined Wade at the food table that groaned beneath the weight of party food. "Happy belated birthday, by the way."

"Aw, thanks. Same to you. And congratulations about you and Nathan." Then he frowned. "How did you know it was my birthday recently?"

"Ben told me. He was shopping for your gift at the time." Shaun couldn't resist. "How was your present, by the way? Once you'd taken the red bow off, of course."

Wade's jaw dropped, and Ben laughed from across the room. "FYI, the bow ended up being rainbow-colored." When Wade gazed at him with narrowed eyes, Ben held his hands high. "Hey, all I told him was, I was buying a bow. I didn't tell him where it was going—his mind did the rest."

"Guys?" Dylan's clear voice rose. "Any of you making a New Year's resolution?"

Mark snorted. "Yeah, I am. I hereby resolve to spend less time at the gym."

Dylan stared at him with raised eyebrows. "It doesn't count when you have a garage full of gym equipment."

"But it's not a gym," Mark said with a smile.

Grammy got up from her chair and went out of the room.

Seb closed the door. "Anyone wanna hear *my* New Year's resolution?" He grinned.

"Oh God," Finn muttered. "Can't wait to hear this."

Seb grabbed Marcus by the arm and pulled him close. "I hereby resolve to get Marcus pregnant."

Cackles erupted from all over the room.

Nathan laughed. "I hate to burst your bubble, and I'm pretty sure I don't need to point this out, but that isn't gonna happen anytime soon."

Seb's eyes twinkled. "Yeah, okay, but think of all the fun I'll have trying." Howls of laughter followed his words.

"I think resolutions are a waste of time," Wade observed. "They're always stuff like, 'I'll eat less' or 'I'll go to the gym more often'. And they're forgotten by the end of January."

"I'll make one," Shaun announced suddenly. When all eyes turned toward him, he took Nathan's hand. "I hereby resolve to make this a happy year."

To his surprise, the others picked up their glasses and raised them.

"This. *So* much this." Noah's voice cracked. "You deserve it."

Shaun's throat seized, and hot tears pricked his eyes.

"Nathan," Finn said in a sing song voice. "That was your cue to kiss him."

Before Shaun could argue that Nathan didn't need a cue, Nathan took him in his arms. "And I resolve to make *you* happy," he whispered before pressing his lips to Shaun's in a chaste kiss. Applause started somewhere, rippling around the room, and swelling until the walls resounded with it.

Nathan released him. "That good enough for ya?" he asked Finn.

"That was perfect." Finn glanced at Joel. "Will you be making any resolutions this year?"

Joel put down his glass, and cleared his throat. "Actually, I don't have a resolution, but a confession."

Finn blinked. "Is this something you can share in polite company? Or in front of these guys," he added with a grin.

Joel sighed. "I lied. I didn't go to see the kids and Laura's new puppy yesterday. I went to Portland to pick something up." Then he lowered himself onto one knee, reaching into the pocket of his jeans.

"Oh God," Finn said weakly. A hush fell over the partygoers.

Joel held out a small black box, in which nestled a gleaming gold band. "I have a question for you. I *was* going to ask you at midnight, but I couldn't wait any longer."

"Ask me, ask me," Finn demanded, one hand pressed against his chest.

Shaun's heart pounded as Joel took Finn's hand in his. "Finn Anderson, will you make me the happiest man on earth, and be my husband?"

Finn hauled Joel to his feet, grabbed his head, and kissed him with a ferocity that took Shaun's breath away. "Yes, yes, yes. Love you so much." Shouts and whoops filled the air, and the pair were surrounded, everyone offering their congratulations.

Grammy appeared in the doorway. "What's going on? Why isn't someone outside to light the fireworks? It's almost midnight."

"I'm going, I'm going!" Noah hurried out of the room.

Shaun and Nathan followed everyone to the French doors in the dining room, where the curtains were already drawn back. While they waited for Grammy to give the signal, Shaun squeezed Nathan's hand.

"Welcome to my family." He smiled. "My ever-growing, very non-traditional family."

Nathan kissed his cheek. "You have two families now." As the countdown reached zero and the first fireworks shot fountains of sparks into the night sky, Nathan took Shaun in his arms. "Happy New Year, baby." He kissed Shaun, a slow lingering kiss that held the promise of more before daylight dawned.

Shaun pulled back and looked him in the eye. "I think you mean, Happy New Life."

The End

<u>Aaron's Awakening</u> (Maine Men Book Six)

Aaron isn't looking for love, but it finds him – and it has a few surprises in store...

A laidback man who goes with the flow
Aaron is happy for his friends who've found love, but he's starting to feel as if he's an endangered species – a single guy. Not that he's looking for anyone. But if someone *were* to turn up, he figures they would be female, younger than his twenty-seven years, and as disinterested as he was in searching for a soul mate.
He's about to get it wrong on most counts.
Working in the Acadia National Park, he meets all kinds of people, like that painter he met the other day. A quiet guy, but he certainly made an impression. Because for some reason, Aaron can't get him out of his mind.

A bruised soul seeking inspiration
Dean has picked up his paintbrush again. A famous artist who's spent the last couple of years producing book illustrations under a different name, he's come back to Maine seeking inspiration – and leaving the past behind him. The glorious natural beauty breathes new life into him, and it brings with it a new friend, a handsome ranger, the only person Dean has felt a connection to in a long time.
But when that connection unexpectedly becomes physical and Dean's emotions get entangled, he fears history is about to repeat itself.
He's not about to let his heart be broken a second time.

THANK YOU

As always, a huge thank you to my beta team. Where would I be without you?

Kazy Reed, you are awesome. Thank you for making sure my boys sound like they're from the USA and not the UK. LOL

And a special thank you to Jason Mitchell. You ROCK. You have so much going on in your own life, and you still find time to talk with me, bounce ideas back and forth... usually before dawn.

Also by K.C. Wells

Learning to Love
Michael & Sean
Evan & Daniel
Josh & Chris
Final Exam

Sensual Bonds
A Bond of Three
A Bond of Truth

Merrychurch Mysteries
Truth Will Out
Roots of Evil
A Novel Murder

Love, Unexpected
Debt
Burden

Dreamspun Desires
The Senator's Secret
Out of the Shadows
My Fair Brady
Under the Covers

Lions & Tigers & Bears
A Growl, a Roar, and a Purr

Love Lessons Learned
First
Waiting for You

Step by Step
Bromantically Yours
BFF

Collars & Cuffs
An Unlocked Heart
Trusting Thomas
Someone to Keep Me (K.C. Wells & Parker Williams)
A Dance with Domination
Damian's Discipline (K.C. Wells & Parker Williams)
Make Me Soar
Dom of Ages (K.C. Wells & Parker Williams)
Endings and Beginnings (K.C. Wells & Parker Williams)

Secrets – with Parker Williams
Before You Break
An Unlocked Mind
Threepeat
On the Same Page

Personal
Making it Personal
Personal Changes
More than Personal
Personal Secrets
Strictly Personal
Personal Challenges
Personal – The complete series

Confetti, Cake & Confessions
(FREE)

Connections
Saving Jason
A Christmas Promise
The Law of Miracles
My Christmas Spirit
A Guy for Christmas
Dear Santa

Island Tales
Waiting for a Prince
September's Tide
Submitting to the Darkness
Island Tales Vol 1 (Books #1 & #2)

Lightning Tales
Teach Me
Trust Me
See Me
Love Me

A Material World
Lace
Satin
Silk
Denim

Southern Boys
Truth & Betrayal
Pride & Protection
Desire & Denial

Maine Men
Finn's Fantasy

Ben's Boss
Seb's Summer
Dylan's Dilemma

Kel's Keeper
Here For You
Sexting The Boss
Gay on a Train
Sunshine & Shadows
Double or Nothing
Back from the Edge
Switching it up
Out for You (FREE)
State of Mind (FREE)
No More Waiting (FREE)
Watch and Learn
My Best Friend's Brother
Princely Submission
Bears in the Woods

Anthologies

Fifty Gays of Shade
Winning Will's Heart

Come, Play
Watch and Learn

Writing as Tantalus
Damon & Pete: Playing with Fire

ABOUT THE AUTHOR

K.C. Wells lives on an island off the south coast of the UK, surrounded by natural beauty. She writes about men who love men, and can't even contemplate a life that doesn't include writing.

The rainbow rose tattoo on her back with the words 'Love is Love' and 'Love Wins' is her way of hoisting a flag. She plans to be writing about men in love - be it sweet or slow, hot or kinky - for a long while to come.

Printed in Great Britain
by Amazon